• World Famous •

STRANGE BUT TRUE

. World Famous .

STRANGE
BUT TRUE

Colin Wilson, Damon Wilson and Rowan Wilson

MAGPIE
London

Magpie Books Ltd
7 Kensington Church Court
London W8 4SP

First published in the UK 1994

ISBN 1 85813 405 6

Typeset by Hewer Text Composition Services, Edinburgh
Printed in Finland by
Werner Söderström Oy

CONTENTS

• chapter one •

STRANGE
VANISHINGS

O *n a warm June Sunday in 1906, a youth named Harold Wilkins
was asked to join a search party for three missing children. That
morning, the three had gone to play in a field near their home, a mile
from Gloucester – a boy, aged ten, and his two sisters, aged three and
five. When they failed to return home for lunch, their father, a railway
brakeman named Vaughan, went to look for them in "Forty Acre"
field; he found no sign of them, so he raised the alarm, and crowds of
neighbours searched the area and the surrounding countryside.*

More than half a century later, Harold Wilkins told the story
in a book called *Mysteries, Solved and Unsolved*: how he and
many others had scoured the field, which was close to the
locomotive-engine shed of the old Midland Railway, and had
failed to find the slightest sign of the children. "Every inch
was probed with sticks ... Had a dead dog been dumped
there, he would certainly have been found." The police came
to the conclusion that the Vaughan children had been
kidnapped, and the following morning newspapers were
full of the story. The Vaughan family received a great deal
of sympathy, and cash donations and postal orders began to
pour into the local post office. Vaughan himself seems to
have been a rather coarse and brutal character, who when the
local vicar called, closed the door in his face with the
comment that he "didn't want no bloody parsons knocking
at his door."

At six a.m. on the following Thursday morning, a ploughman starting work in a nearby field looked over a hedge and
saw the three children fast asleep in a ditch. They were
quickly restored to their parents, and newspaper readers
awaited the solution of the mystery with interest. They were
disappointed. The children had no idea of what all the fuss
was about, and no idea that they had been missing for three
days. The Superintendent of the Gloucester police, Nehemiah
Philpott, took the view that the ploughman had kidnapped
the children for ransom, and refused to hand over a penny of
the reward money, which had been donated by readers of the
News of the World. But local reporters only had to look at the
labourer's cottage – in the nearby hamlet of Coney Hill – to
see that this could not be true; it was tiny, and so close to
neighbouring cottages that it would have been impossible to
smuggle a cat in without being noticed. Besides, the ploughman had been gathering in the harvest at the time the
children had vanished.

When Wilkins told the story in 1959, the eldest of the missing
children was still alive, and verified that he did not have the
slightest recollection of what happened in the four days during
which hundreds of people were searching. It is true that the
ditch where they were found might have been overlooked. But
would three children sleep straight through four days?

Wilkins has his own theory about the mystery. He
suggests that certain places on earth – places associated
with witchcraft and ancient rites – are pervaded by strange
unknown forces, and that such forces may not be limited by
our normal space–time dimensions. But whether or not we
can accept the "strange forces" theory, the fact remains that
there have been hundreds of similar "vanishings" – so many
that whole books have been devoted to them. And many
cases involve people who have disappeared "into thin air".
On 3 September 1873, an athletically inclined shoemaker
named James Burne Worson bet three friends that he could
run from Leamington to Coventry, in Warwickshire (a
distance of forty miles). The friends followed him in a
cart. A few miles along the road, Worson stumbled, fell
headlong, and disappeared. His friends – including Burns, a
photographer, and Wise, a linen-draper – insisted that he
did not even touch the ground. Worson was never found.
Neither was a seven-year-old boy named Denis Martin, who
was walking within sight of his father and other adults in

the Great Smoky Mountains in the summer of 1969, when he simply vanished.

These are two of the rare cases in which the vanishing was witnessed. Far more frequent are cases like that of Sherman Church, reported in the *Chicago Tribune* for 5 January 1900.

"Sherman Church, a young man employed in the Augusta Mills (Battle Creek, Mich.) has disappeared. He was seated in the Company's office, when he arose and ran into the mill. He has not been seen since. The mill has been almost taken to pieces by the searchers, and the river, woods and country have been scoured, but to no avail. Nobody saw Church leave town, nor is there any known reason for his doing so." This case is one of many collected by an American historian of the weird and inexplicable, Charles Fort, who – as we shall see – is the patron saint of such events.

How could a human being vanish "into thin air"? The American broadcaster Long John Nebel has a highly circumstantial account of how it happened before the eyes of a whole audience, in New York's Paramount Theatre. During a Thursday afternoon matinee, Nebel's friend William Neff, a well-known conjuror, stepped into a spotlight in front of the curtain and began his patter. As Nebel watched, it seemed to him that he could see light through Neff's body, as if he were turning into frosted glass. Slowly, Neff became transparent, then disappeared completely, although his voice continued to sound perfectly normal. After a while, a faint outline "like a very fine pencil sketch" began to appear; a few minutes later, Neff was back again, looking perfectly normal. The audience seems to have assumed that the vanishing was a part of his act. As soon as the show was over, Nebel rushed backstage to ask how Neff had done it. Neff seemed surprised; he was not aware that he had "faded". But he admitted that the same thing had happened three years earlier at a theatre in Chicago. Moreover, it had happened only a few evenings before as he sat watching television with his wife Evelyn. He had been alerted to the fact that something was wrong when his wife had screamed. When Neff went over and touched her, she screamed again and said: "Who's touching me?" He then hastened from the room to get her a glass of water, and when he returned, she flung her arms round him and said: "I was so frightened – I couldn't see you for a few minutes." Evelyn was so upset that Neff forbade Nebel to question her about it. And Nebel, who tells the story in his book *The Way Out World*, can offer no explanation.

Around the turn of the twentieth century, there were a number of theorists who thought they knew the answer. After the invention of non-Euclidean geometry by mathematicians like Riemann and Lobachevsky, many scientists became convinced that there must exist a "fourth dimension" at right angles to the other three (length, breadth and height), and that it is merely the limitations of the human mind that prevent us from seeing it. And a Professor Johann C.F. Zollner of Leipzig University suspected that this must be the answer to some of the more baffling questions of psychical research – for example, how the mysterious entity named the poltergeist (also known as the banging ghost) can sometimes throw objects *through* solid walls. (His suggestion was that the objects don't go "through", but into the fourth dimension and out again, just as a giant could step over a wall that would be unscalable to a tortoise.) In 1877, Professor Zollner convinced a large number of sceptics with an interesting experiment with a spiritualist "medium" named Henry Slade.

While the medium was in a trance, the "spirits" were asked to tie a knot in a circular piece of cord, and they obliged by doing so without breaking the cord. Unbelievers suggested that the medium had merely switched cords, but Zollner insisted that his test conditions were too tight for that.

A Russian philosopher named P.D. Ouspensky became so fascinated by the fourth dimension that he devoted most of his first book to this subject. And in *Tertium Organum*, he reports that Johan Van Manen, a scientist, described how, one night, as he lay in bed trying to visualise the fourth dimension, "I plainly saw before me first a four-dimensional globe and afterwards a four-dimensional cube . . ." Unless Van Manen was deceiving himself (although he claimed to be able to recall the globe with ease, and the cube with some difficulty) then our minds *are* capable of grasping that extra dimension. Ouspensky argued that the fourth dimension is the key to a proper understanding of the universe. For example, our three-dimensional understanding cannot grasp the idea of the universe having a beginning or an end, but insight into the fourth dimension would probably allow us to. Albert Einstein – who was unknown at this time – later argued that the fourth dimension is actually time, and spoke of the universe as being a kind of "finite yet unbounded" space which curves into the fourth dimension like a sphere.

Ambrose Bierce

Among all these speculations, Zollner's experiment stands out as a genuinely useful insight. For there can be no possible doubt about the real existence of poltergeists – there are literally thousands of recorded examples of these mischievous "spirits" that throw things and make appalling rackets. Many modern researchers are convinced that poltergeists are a strange effect of the unconscious mind – particularly, disturbed adolescents' minds – and they prefer to speak of "spontaneous psychokinesis" (i.e. mind over matter).

Others believe that poltergeists are some kind of spirit. But most accept the evidence that poltergeists can cause water to spill out of sealed pipes, and throw objects out of locked rooms through solid walls or doors. The existence of a fourth dimension is the only sensible hypothesis that can explain these phenomena.

In recent years, Harold Wilkins' "strange forces" theory has received some interesting support from students of terrestrial magnetism. Everybody knows that the earth is a magnet; nobody knows why. But zoologists have now established that birds migrate by following lines of the earth's magnetic force, and that animals use them too, for "homing".

"Dowsers" (water diviners) are also sensitive to these lines of

---

People in the Welsh town of Wrexham and the surrounding countryside were startled to see hay flying under its own power one ordinary summer day in the late nineteenth century.

According to an account carried in the newspaper, the event occurred at 2 p.m. on a calm July day.

Suddenly some haymakers on a farm saw about half a ton of hay sailing above them through the sky. They said it was higher than they had even seen a crow fly.

The flying hay moved in a northerly direction, which was somewhat surprising because it was going against the wind. Although the mass separated slowly as it covered more distance, it travelled at least five miles without falling apart entirely. It had risen from a field about five miles from Wrexham and had flown over that town at some point in its flight. As the article said, "it caused much consternation while passing over the town."

At the end of this flight of hay, wisps lay here and there along its route. One large clump fell in the middle of a field some distance from the point at which the half-ton mass had first taken to the sky.

"earth force". Soon after the Second World War, Guy Under-
wood, a retired solicitor, decided to devote his remaining days to
exploring prehistoric sites with a dowsing rod. He quickly
discovered that all prehistoric sites had at their centres "blind
springs", from which streams radiated. The electrical forces of
the earth in these places take the form of a huge spiral.
(Significantly, "spiral" carvings can be found on all kinds of
ancient stones at sacred sites.) Stonehenge, for example, presents
a mass of these spirals and loops; the site was obviously chosen
for a pagan temple because Stone Age priests could sense that
there was something strange and powerful about the earth there.
Moreover, when Christianity replaced paganism, Christian
churches were deliberately built on sites of pagan temples, as
if the builders were aware that the ground itself is "sacred".

One of the odd things about such sites is that the sites
themselves seem to be able to "record" human emotions. It
seems probable that many a "haunted" house is simply a house
where a tragedy has taken place and where the earth forces
have somehow "recorded" the negative emotions. Sensitive
people often experience a "creepy feeling" in such places. One
dowser, Paul Devereux, visited the Rollright Stones, near
Oxford, after a black magic group had performed ceremonies
there (including animal sacrifice); he said that the place posi-
tively reeked of "nastiness", which it took days of ceremonial
cleansing to remove.

It has to be admitted that for some cases of mysterious
"vanishings" there is a simpler explanation. One of the best
known is that of a farmer called David Lang who, on the
afternoon of 23 September 1880, strolled across a field by his
home near Gallatin, Tennessee, in full view of his family, and
vanished into thin air. A friend approaching the farm in a
buggy saw Lang wave to him a second before he disappeared.
Five people rushed to the spot where he had vanished,
expecting to find a hole; but the ground was solid. Lang
was never found, and the story, reported in many American
newspapers, caused a sensation.

Unfortunately, the story was untrue. After reporting it in a
book called *Enigmas and Mysteries*, I decided to try and get some
more detail, and asked a friend in Tennessee to investigate. She
did – and learned that a hardware salesman, Joe McHatten,
having spent a boring day in Gallatin confined to his room by
snow, had whiled away the time by writing his wife a letter in
which he had invented the whole story.

Disappointing. But, according to an American historian of the bizarre named Robert Jay Nash (who recounts the case in *Among the Missing*), it was based on a real occurrence that took place a quarter of a century earlier. In July 1854, Orion Williamson, a farmer of Selma, Alabama, was strolling across a field to greet two friends who were approaching in a buggy, when he simply vanished. The friends, together with the farmer's frantic wife, searched the field without success. Later that day, three hundred men from Selma examined every inch of the field. They never found Orion Williamson. But the following spring, there was a fifteen-foot circle of dead grass at the spot where Orion Williamson had vanished.

Many years later, the story was retold in the *Cincinnati Enquirer*, where it was read by the American journalist Ambrose Bierce, famous for his horror stories and his mordant sense of humour; he made it the basis of a story entitled "The Difficulty of Crossing a Field". Bierce then went on to to achieve posthumous notoriety by vanishing into thin air – although not, in this case, in front of witnesses.

As Bierce approached the age of seventy – he was born in 1842 – he became increasingly cantankerous and restive. In his heyday he had been a famous wit and, virtually, the literary dictator of San Francisco; the thought of succumbing to decay enraged him. His life had been adventurous and tragic – one son had committed suicide and another died of drink – and there is evidence that he himself planned to die with his boots on. In 1913, he decided to revisit the battlefields of the Civil War – in which he had fought with distinction – then go on to Mexico, where there was also a civil war, and perhaps to South America. In fact, Bierce so impressed the Mexican bandit-turned-revolutionary, Pancho Villa, that Villa issued the writer with credentials to accompany him as a war correspondent. Bierce's last letter was written from Chihuahua, Mexico, on 26 December 1913. Then came silence. Ever since that time, "investigators" have produced "authentic" accounts of what happened. One declared that Bierce had lost his temper with Villa and told him he was nothing but a cutthroat, whereupon Villa had instantly ordered his execution. Another said that he had been killed in the siege of Ojinago, and that his death had been reported in Mexican army dispatches. One of his friends in Washington always insisted that he had blown out his brains on a high ledge of the Grand Canyon and them fallen into its depths ("an appropriate tombstone for his gigantic ego"). But the most bizarre story is that he had been captured by a wild tribe in southern Mexico and boiled alive, after which his shrunken remains had been worshipped. This is, clearly, the version that Bierce himself would have chosen.

chapter two

THE MAN WHO LOVED MYSTERIES

C harles Hoy Fort, the patron saint of the inexplicable, was a hermit and an intellectual rebel who died in New York City in 1932 at the age of fifty-seven.

Charles Fort's father was a wealthy businessman who ruled his family with autocratic severity, often beating Charles with a dog-whip. An intelligent and strong-willed child, Fort grew up with a passionate hatred of authority and stupidity. He was always a maverick.

He had always wanted to be a naturalist, and was an eager collector of specimens. But in his teens he decided to be a writer and took a job on the Albany *Democrat*. He wrote novels – three and a half million words according to his own later estimate – but only one was published. It was a flop. Perhaps it was because Fort writes in a series of brief flat statements, often without verbs. To say that his style lacks flow and readability is an understatement.

In his late teens he travelled around the world on an allowance of $25 a month. After his trip, he married an English girl, and settled in a cheap apartment in New York. He made a poor living from journalism. Later, he received a small income from securities, but life was always a struggle. Fort was an eccentric and a recluse, obsessed by the mysterious and the unexplained from a fairly early age. He devoured books on Atlantis, the hollow earth theory, and the mystery of the pyramids. One of his own earliest books argued that our civilization is secretly controlled from Mars. He called this book simply X. Subsequently he wrote a book called Y, and planned another called Z.

Fort himself was no crank, however. He wrote X and Y with tongue in cheek, but later he attempted a closely reasoned statement of his beliefs in *The Book of the Damned*, published in 1919. By "damned" he meant phenomena that had been discredited and disregarded by orthodox science – enigmas, unsolved mysteries, the unexplained.

Here is a typical Fort entry:

> Extract from the log of the bark *Lady of the Lake* by Captain F.W. Banner: . . .
>
> "That upon the 22nd of March, 1870, at Lat. 5° 47′ N., Long. 27° 52′ W., the sailors of the *Lady of the Lake* saw a remarkable object, or "cloud", in the sky. They reported to the captain.
>
> According to Capt. Banner, it was a cloud of circular form, with an included semicircle divided into four parts, the central dividing shaft beginning

---

An earthquake. A deluge of rain. Dead fish in dried up pools all over town. This weird sequence of events happened in Singapore in 1861. The description of it in *La Science Pour Tous* said the fish had not fallen with the rain. The local inhabitants of Singapore said they had. Charles Fort, American writer on the occult, supported the view that the fish had fallen from the sky. He thought "that a whole lakeful of them [fish] had been shaken down from the Super-Sargasso Sea."

Fort spent his life collecting scraps of information about odd, hard-to-explain occurrences everywhere in the world. He used such bits in his various books, which he wrote as his personal protest against modern science's failure to deal with psychic phenomena.

In *The Book of the Damned*, published in 1919, Fort talks about Singapore's puddles of fish as an example of things falling from the sky. He says that many such falling objects come from the Super-Sargasso Sea. According to Fort, this sea is a "region somewhere above the earth's surface in which gravitation is inoperative . . ." He goes on to say, "I think that things raised from this earth's surface to that region have been held there until shaken down by storms.

at the center of the circle and extending far outward, and then curving backward.

Geometricity and complexity and stability of form: and the small likelihood of a cloud maintaining such diversity of features, to say nothing of appearance of organic form.

Light gray in color, or it was cloud-color.

That whatever it may have been, it traveled against the wind . . .

For half an hour this form was visible. When it did finally disappear that was not because it disintegrated like a cloud, but because it was lost to sight in the evening darkness.

This might make the reader think at once of a flying saucer, especially since Captain Banner's description sounds like hundreds of other UFO sightings. But Fort recorded this account in 1918, thirty years before the start of the UFO craze. He was merely quoting from the *Journal of the Royal Meteorological Society*, an eminently respectable publication. He makes no attempts to draw conclusions from the report. It is simply one of hundreds of similar unexplainable occurrences that he quotes at length and in detail.

We can see immediately why Fort's contemporaries regarded him as mildly if not certifiably insane. Fort spent thirty years of his life in the New York Public Library, searching through piles of old newspapers and magazines for items like the one quoted above. He was particularly fond of tales of odd things falling from the sky – frogs, fish, blood, and snowflakes two-feet square. But what did it all add up to? Why should Fort spend a lifetime assembling a vast collection of tall stories and make no attempt to tie them together into a theory?

The flying saucer story above provides the answer. Fort could be described as a man of inspired intuition. He was also, by upbringing and training, a typical product of the age that believed in hard work, sound common sense, and respect for authority. All his instincts told him there was something wrong with the neat and orderly universe of science, and that the actual universe was a million times stranger than even the most brilliant scientist of his day could imagine. It was this instinct that rang a bell when he read the flying saucer story and dozens more like it – although he would have found it difficult to explain precisely why. In a sense, he wasn't even interested in explaining these phenomena. He felt there could be dozens of possible explanations, all equally at variance with scientific thinking, all equally exciting and fruitful.

Here is a typical example of the kind of thing that interested him. On 28 July 1860, fifteen years before Fort's birth, a great meteorite covered with ice crashed down in Dhurmsalla, India. The event was duly noted and described by a trustworthy authority, the British Deputy Commissioner in the area. An ice-covered meteorite is certainly strange, since most meteorites are white hot from tearing through our atmosphere. That was not all. On the next evening the Commissioner saw lights in the sky, some of them fairly low. They moved around like fire balloons. Nowadays we would probably assume they were the lights of airplanes, but this was long before the invention of the airplane. Fort also noticed from the Commissioner's report that other unusual events had occurred around the same time in India. Newspapers had reported a shower of live fish at Benares, a fall of some red substance at Farrukhabad, a dark spot observed on the sun, an earthquake, a lengthy period of darkness during daylight hours, and a luminous effect in the sky like the aurora borealis.

In the following year on 16 February 1861 there was an earthquake in Singapore, followed by a tremendous storm with three days of torrential rain. The odd thing was that in the pools of water formed by the rain, fish were seen swimming around; and when the pools dried up, dead fish were found on the ground. The most popular theory was that the heavy rain had caused a river to overflow, spreading the fish over a wide area. However, a reporter of the event recorded that fish were found in his courtyard, which was surrounded by a high wall that kept the water out.

Here Fort offers a strange, mixed mass of data, some baffling, some fairly straightforward. There is nothing unusual in a sun-spot, or in the aurora borealis effect that followed it. The lights in the sky could in fact have been fire balloons or ball lightning, although the Commissioner stated that he was sure they weren't. As to the rain of red substance and the falling fish, it seems just conceivable that they were carried aloft by a whirlpool or waterspout. Fort agrees that all these explanations could be true, but argues that there must be something more when so many strange events occur together. "My own acceptance is that either a world or a vast super-construction . . . hovered over India in the summer of 1860," he says. As to

Paul Trent of Oregon, photographed a flying saucer cruising silently over his farm in 1948.

the lights in the sky, his suggestion is: "Visitors." One of his general conclusions is that the earth has had many "visitors" at various times in its history. As to what kind of visitors: "I can think of as many different kinds of visitors to this earth as there are visitors to New York, to a jail, to a church – some people go to church to pick pockets."

Fort likes to keep all his options open. That is why he refuses to commit himself to any single theory to explain all the strange events he writes about. He always has half a dozen possible solutions for everything. Perhaps our earth passed through an area of space where there were shattered fragments of some other world. Perhaps "super-vehicles" have travelled through our atmosphere. (This seems to make Fort the inventor of the UFO hypothesis.) Perhaps there is some *other* world – a kind of twin to this one – in another dimension. Or perhaps all these theories are wide of the mark, and the truth is that "all things are phantoms in a super-mind in a dreaming state." Just as you are beginning to feel that perhaps Fort is building up to some plausible scientific theory after all, he reaches into his hat like a conjuror and produces some new and even more outrageous hypothesis. For example, he suggests that human beings may be "property" belonging to some invisible super-farmer. He seems to *want* his readers to lose patience and throw the book across the room.

As could be expected, most of Fort's contemporaries ignored him, and he repaid their neglect with contempt. When the writer Tiffany Thayer launched a Fortean Society in his honour, Fort firmly declined to become a member. He probably feared that his disciples would try to pin him down to a definite set of ideas and beliefs, and he had no intention of being pinned down.

For day after day and year after year, Fort continued his obsessive search through the world's newspapers, making endless notes on slips of paper which he kept in shoe boxes. After *The Book of the Damned* came *New Lands*, then *Lo!*, and finally *Wild Talents*. Fort became more and more of a hermit. He spent the morning in the library, and the afternoon at his desk, working in a small dark room that overlooked a courtyard. Almost his only recreation was going to the movies in the neighbourhood four or five times a week, and he said he went to keep his wife company. For himself, most films "bored him to death."

While Fort was writing *Wild Talents* his health began to break down – understandably, in view of his dreary and frustrating existence. He wrote desperately, often sending his wife to the movies alone and joining her later. The recluse became intensely resentful of all visitors, refusing to see anyone. He would not even consult a doctor. Finally, Fort became so weak that his wife had to send for an ambulance and take him to the hospital. But he had finished his book. When the publisher brought a copy of *Wild Talents* to the hospital, Fort was too weak to hold it. He died later the same day.

Fort was ignored in death as in life. Although the Fortean Society continued, it was composed of a small group of eccentrics. They admired Fort's fierce individualism, but if members of the general public picked up Fort's books, they soon dropped them again. Fort seldom bothers to tell a complete story. He breaks off halfway through some anecdote about giants or fairies or spontaneous combustion to denounce orthodox scientists or to hector the reader. He simply dumps his many facts like a cartload of stones, and leaves the reader to sort them out. This may be why Fort remained unread, and almost unremembered, for a quarter of a century after his death.

An event of 1947 led to Fort's resurrection. In that year an American businessman flying his private plane near Mount Rainier, Washington, saw nine gleaming disks hurtling at tremendous speed through the sky. Within months many more sightings of flying saucers had been reported, and within a few years there were thousands of reports from all over the world. Even then, few people remembered Fort, pioneer of the UFO idea. In France, however, Fort had at least one ardent admirer. This was Jacques Bergier, a student of philosophy and occultism. Bergier was fascinated by unexplained enigmas such as the riddle of the pyramids, the Easter Island statues, and evidence for highly evolved civilizations in the remote past. In the late 1950s Bergier teamed up with a brilliant journalist, Louis Pauwels, and together they produced the book that Fort had attempted to write all his life. They called it *The Morning of the Magicians*. When it appeared in Paris in 1960, it became an immediate best-seller. It contained a chapter about Charles Fort, and acknowledged its indebtedness to him. Published in Britain and the United States in 1963, it inspired hundreds of imitators. Secondhand works on Atlantis, magic, pyramidology, alchemy, and astrology began to get record prices. Publishers realized there was an "occult boom," and began to flood the market with titles like *World of the Weird* and *Nothing So Strange*. All Fort's books were reissued in paperback, and translations appeared all over the world. Recognition had finally arrived – half a century too late.

Many people now regard Fort as a prophet and a visionary, and many of his ideas have become part of the intellectual currency of our time. Today we freely discuss the possibility of a multidimensional universe in which other worlds could exist parallel with ours. The idea of visitors from other worlds has become commonplace in the past two decades. Arthur C. Clarke's *2001* suggested that human evolution may have been aided by beings from another galaxy – an idea that has become part of contemporary mythology. The Russian philosopher Georgei Gurdjieff, who has attained the status of a cult figure, liked to describe human beings as hypnotized sheep kept stupid and contented by some magician until it is time for the slaughter house. Another cult figure, the Argentinian writer and Nobel Prize winner Jorge Luis Borges, has often speculated that human beings are dreams in the mind of God – and that perhaps God himself is a dream in some even more civilized mind. In recent years, some scientists have suggested that there could be another universe of "antimatter" in which the atoms would be made up of antiprotons, antineutrons, and antielectrons. If ever such a universe were to come into contact with our own, there would be a dull explosion – and then Nothing.

Fort once said that every science is a mutilated octopus. "If its tentacles were not clipped to stumps, it would feel its way into disturbing contacts." Sixty years after the death of Charles Fort, it seems that we may at last be entering the age of what he called disturbing contacts.

chapter three

MORE UNEXPLAINED DISAPPEARANCES

In December 1937 China and Japan had been at war for six months, and the Chinese were getting the worst of the struggle. Shanghai fell, and in spite of the protests of the League of Nations, the Japanese advanced on the capital of Nanking.

South of the city, the Chinese commander Colonel Li Fu Sien decided to make a last-ditch stand in the low hills. An urgent request brought over 3000 reinforcements. The colonel disposed these troops in a two-mile line, close to an important bridge across the Yangtze River. They had a quantity of heavy artillery, and were prepared for a life-and-death struggle. The colonel returned to his headquarters a mile behind the lines, and waited for the Japanese attack. At dawn he was awakened by his aide, who told him that they were unable to contact the army. Had they been overrun by the Japanese in the night? The colonel and an escort drove cautiously toward the right flank to investigate. To their amazement the positions were deserted. The guns were still in position – but the men had vanished. Further investigation revealed that a small pocket of soldiers, about a hundred, were still encamped near the bridge. They had heard no sounds in the night. If the army had deserted or surrendered to the Japanese, they would have had to pass close to the camp. The sentries on the bridge also testified that no one had crossed the bridge in the night.

It was preposterous. Three thousand men cannot vanish into

thin air. Even if they had all deserted, such a mass exodus would have been bound to attract attention. Yet no one had heard or seen anything.

The Chinese had little time to ponder the problem. The Japanese army advanced across the river, and two days later Nanking fell. There followed one of the most horrifying and cruel massacres in history – the "rape of Nanking". The atrocities were so appalling that three Japanese commanders were recalled to Japan, as were many soldiers. The "vanishing army" ceased to be a matter of central importance to the Chinese generals. But it was generally expected that the mystery would be solved when peace returned – that perhaps the solution lay in the records of the Japanese

Walter Powell was an English politician who was the Member of Parliament for a Wiltshire area. On 1 December 1881 he became part of an unsolved mystery when he went up in a balloon with two of his friends. They came down on a beach in Dorset, the two got out, and Powell started to follow. Suddenly the balloon gave a violent jerk and went high up into the clouds again with Powell still on board. He was never seen again.

It seemed likely that he might have crashed into the English Channel, and a search was made for three days. The beaches on England's southern coast were combed for clues night and day. Nothing helpful turned up anywhere.

Right after Powell's disappearance, reports of mystifying lights and objects in the sky came from England, France, Scotland, and Spain. The day after Powell and the balloon had vanished, people in Dartmouth Harbor saw "two strange bright lights in the sky." Two days later an unidentified luminous object was seen traversing the sky over Cherbourg, France.

On 15 December a ship's captain saw a glowing object in the sky. He described it as the "gondola of a balloon, which seemed alternately to increase and diminish in size." That was in the east of Scotland. On the 16th, three Spanish coastguards reported seeing something that looked like a balloon in the sky. They climbed the nearby mountain to investigate, and saw it shoot out sparks as it vanished. The next day about seventy-five miles east of this sighting, a similar and strangely glowing object was reported.

Could these unusual sightings have had a connection with Powell's lost balloon?

army. In fact, the Japanese army reports contained no mention of the missing 3000 men. Today they are regarded as mysterious casualties of war. But no one knows what became of them.

Why has this mystery failed to excite more attention? The answer is probably that the misery and chaos of the Sino–Japanese war made it seem unimportant. The same seems to apply to an equally strange event that took place during World War I.

In April 1915 Allied armies landed on the Gallipoli Peninsula in European Turkey in an attempt to capture what was then the capital of the Turkish Empire (now Istanbul). They wanted to make contact with Russian allies through the Black Sea. It was bad strategy. Turkish resistance was stubborn, and the Allies were forced to withdraw nine months later, having lost hundreds of thousands of men.

Some of the bloodiest fighting in Gallipoli took place around a spot called Hill 60 near Suvla Bay. On the morning of 28 August 1915 a British regiment, the First Fourth Norfolk, prepared to attack Hill 60. The regiment consisted of more than a thousand men. It was a warm, clear day, but several observers remember noticing a group of curious low clouds over Hill 60. Although there was a breeze, these clouds seemed to remain stationary. The observers reported watching the regiment march uphill until the entire file of men disappeared into one of these "loaf shaped" clouds. Then the clouds moved away – leaving no sign of the army.

The disappearance of the regiment was duly reported to the British Government by the Commander-in-Chief of the Allied Expeditionary Force in Gallipoli. He made no mention of the mysterious clouds, but reported that the regiment had separated from the main body of troops and had vanished. The whole regiment was subsequently posted as "missing" – the assumption being that all its men had either been killed or taken prisoner. When the war ended in 1918 the British asked the Turks about their missing regiment. The Turks replied that they knew nothing about it. Their armies had never made contact with the First Fourth Norfolk.

In 1920 the bodies of a number of soldiers belonging to the First Fourth Norfolk were found in Gallipoli. It was assumed that these men must have died in battle after all, and that the remainder of the regiment probably perished in Turkish prisoner-of-war camps. Today it is generally accepted that the men of

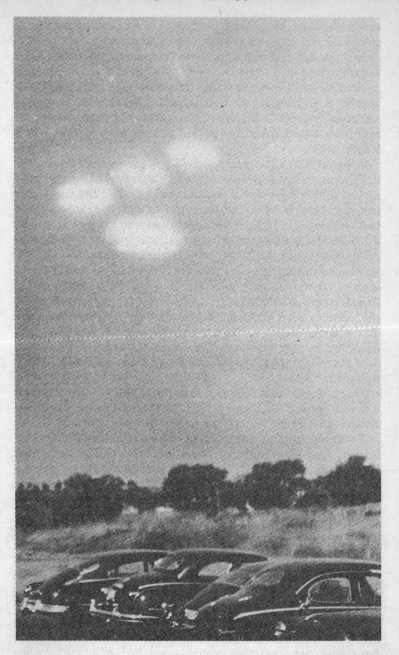

Lights flying in formation above the air station, Salem, USA, 1952

the First Fourth Norfolk were victims of a bloody campaign in which all too many men were lost without trace.

Some people, however, have never accepted this explanation – particularly the witnesses who recalled the strange clouds over Hill 60. The French writer Jacques Vallée was sufficiently curious to investigate the matter, and included the incident in his book *Passport to Magonia*. He used a letter signed by three witnesses attesting to the curious disappearance of the whole regiment into a cloud.

Vallée is a scientist connected with Northwestern University in Chicago. He has also written one of the most balanced books on Unidentified Flying Objects, *Anatomy of a phenomenon*. Vallée puts forward the idea that the regiment marched into a cloud that concealed a UFO. This view is supported by the distinguished British ufologist Brinsley Le Poer Trench, now the Earl of Clancarty, who is Chairman of the International UFO Movement. Le Poer Trench cites another cloud disappearance in the curious case of Dr and Mrs Gerardo Vidal. They were driving home from a family reunion in Chascomus, Argentina, when they drove into a thick cloud of mist. They fell unconscious – and woke to find themselves on a road near Mexico City, 4500 miles away. On telephoning friends in Argentina, they discovered that they had apparently lost two days since they left the party.

This is not the only case in which couples have been *teleported* – that is, moved from one place to another by psychic means – to Mexico. Marcilo Ferraz, the owner of a sugar firm in Brazil, was driving with his wife from São Paulo to Uruguay. Near the border they drove into a white cloud; they woke up to find themselves in Mexico. In 1968 a Brazilian couple, driving through the state of Rio Grande do Sul on their honeymoon, suddenly became extremely drowsy. When they woke up, they were in Mexico.

At this point it is worth mentioning the strange experience of Betty and Barney Hill. It aroused widespread interest, and was the subject of a book, *The Interrupted Journey*, by John G. Fuller. Driving from Canada to New Hampshire in September 1961, the Hills saw a bright object like a star descending through the sky. Looking at the object through binoculars, Barney Hill thought it to be some kind of spacecraft. The couple drove off at high speed, but began to feel drowsy. They woke up an hour later, with no memory of what had happened in the meantime.

When they realized that they had apparently lost an hour –
not to mention thirty-five miles – the Hills feared that they were
going insane and began consulting doctors. Dr Benjamin Si-
mons, a neurosurgeon, helped them recall what had happened
during the lost hour by hypnotizing each of them. Their stories
under hypnosis were the same. The engine of the Hills' car had
failed on the approach of a UFO. They had been taken aboard
the craft by beings unlike humans, and had each been subjected
to a medical examination. Finally they had been put back in
their car, further along the road, with the memory of what had
taken place erased from their consciousness.

The story told by the Hills is supported by medical evidence,
so it seems unlikely that they were lying. On the other hand, it
is possible that the story they told under hypnosis may have
been the product of subconscious fantasy – a kind of dream. A
couple driving a long distance throughout the night are likely
to become drowsy and it might seem to them to have lost
minutes or even hours. It is true that the Hills were hypnotized
separately; but it is conceivable that they had discussed the
possibility of being kidnapped by extraterrestrial beings before
they consulted Dr Simon, and under hypnosis produce a story
based on their discussion. In short, the flying saucer theory
remains no more than a hypothesis to explain these strange
cases of teleportation even though it seems as plausible as any
other hypothesis.

One curious aspect of teleportation incidents is that they so
often involve couples. I have myself discussed such an experience with a couple that went through it – Dr Arthur Guirdham,
former Consultant Psychiatrist to the Bath Medical Area in
southwest England, and his wife Mary. The Guirdhams were
taking a vacation on the Yorkshire moors, and were staying at a
hotel in a small town. One day they visited a town some fifteen
miles away. At the end of the outing, they started to drive back
to their hotel. It was a warm pleasant evening, and they drove
slowly. They had only been driving for five minutes when
Guirdham noticed a signpost that indicated they were only
three miles from their destination. This was clearly impossible
unless they had been driving at more than a hundred miles an
hour. They stopped to consult a map to see if they had taken a
short cut or mistaken the distance. They had not. If the signpost
were right, then they had covered twelve miles in less than five
minutes. And the signpost was right. A few miles further on the
Guirdhams entered the town where their hotel was situated.

There is a matter-of-factness about this story that argues for its truth. Guirdham did not attempt to draw any conclusions from the incident, or use it as the foundation for an argument about time. He simply recounted it as something odd that had once happened to him. His wife Mary confirmed it.

In this case, there was no question of lost time; it was only the distance that had apparently been telescoped. Which brings us to a fundamental question: is it conceivable that space and time could be stretched or compressed like a piece of chewing gum? This is a question that will be raised by many of the enigmas and mysteries recounted in this book, and it may be as well to consider it a little more closely.

In his famous book *An Experiment With Time*, first published in 1927, the British aeronautical engineer J.W. Dunne described how he began having dreams of the future. Among them were dreams of newspaper headlines that appeared the day after he dreamed them. Dunne decided to make a habit of jotting down his dreams when he awoke during the night because he was convinced that many interesting dreams are simply forgotten by the time we wake up in the morning. His records confirmed

It was a bright October morning in 1593. On the plaza in front of the palace in Mexico City there was the usual bustle of people and soldiers. One of these army men stood out. He wore a resplendent uniform unlike the others, and he carried a different kind of gun.

When questioned later, the strange soldier said that his orders that morning were to mount guard at the governor's palace in Manila, where he was stationed. "I know very well this is not the governor's palace – and evidently I am not in Manila," he said ... "But here I am and this is a palace of some kind so I am doing my duty as nearly as possible." The soldier also told the authorities that the governor had been killed the night before.

The soldier couldn't believe that he was thousands of miles away from Manila, and everyone was baffled by his overnight transportation to Mexico City. The man with this incredible tale was put in jail.

Two months afterward a ship arrived from the Philippines. It brought news that the governor had been murdered – on the night before the soldier had appeared. The soldier was released and sent back to Manila. Some 400 years later his marvellous trip through space and time remains a mystery.

that he often dreamed of events which later happened. He persuaded others to write down their dreams, and they also found that they dreamed of future events that came true. As a result of these experiences, Dunne formulated his theory of "serial time". He suggested that there are several different kinds of time, and several different "me"s on different levels of being. For example, there is the superficial "me" who runs to catch trains, and chats with people at parties; a deeper "me" who appreciates music and poetry; and a still deeper "me" who may be aroused by some great crisis or challenge; and so on. Each of these "me"s, Dunne suggests, may have a different kind of time. A simple way to grasp this idea would be to imagine a carousel that contains several different carousels one inside the other, with each one going at a different speed: a different "you" exists on each of the carousels. Because of the speed differences, the "you" on an inner carousel may actually be ahead of the "you" on the outer carousel. Therefore you know what will happen tomorrow, or next week, or even next year.

Dunne's theory has been strongly criticized by many scientists and parapsychologists. Nevertheless it does seem to fit in with those strange glimpses into the future that provide such a challenge to investigators of psychic phenomena. A simple version of Dunne's theory is that time is like a phonograph record, and our human consciousness is like the needle that has to track it. Occasionally the needle can skip a groove, or even several grooves, and jump into the future.

There seems to be a likely possibility that time may be more complex than it looks. But how about space? All our experience tells us that space is the same everywhere. Things *in* space can change, but isn't space itself unchangeable?

The idea of unchangeable space was first challenged in the early years of the twentieth century by Albert Einstein. Although it has been said that only a handful of people fully understand Einstein's Theory of Relativity, its implications caught the imagination of the whole world. The first part of Einstein's theory, the Special Theory of Relativity, was published in 1905. It was concerned with bodies travelling at speeds that approached the enormous speed of light. At such speeds, Einstein suggested, measurements of distance and time would be altered: objects would shrink in length and time would slow down. For instance, a spaceship travelling at half the speed of light – about 93,000 miles per second – would have

only about eighty-five per cent of its length when at rest, and
clocks on board would run at eighty-five per cent of their
normal rate. The crew inside the spaceship would even age
more slowly because the clocks were slowed down. The crew
would not be aware of these effects, however, because everything on the spaceship would be equally affected. On the other
hand, the crew looking at the Earth would find that *it* was
contracted, and would assume that Earth clocks were running
slow compared with theirs. Time slows down on a moving
object, and speeds, time intervals, and length are relative to the
observer who is measuring them, said Einstein.

The effects of motion on the measurements of time and
distance cannot be detected at everyday speeds, but it is
impossible for a human being to move at anything like the
speed of light. In 1961, however, scientists in Geneva succeeded in accelerating a tiny particle called a *meson* to three-
quarters of the speed of light. The usual lifespan of this
particle, when at rest, is only two-millionths of a second;
but at three-quarters of the speed of light, the meson lasted
three-millionths of a second, or half again as long. This
experiment justified Einstein's conclusion that time slows
down on a moving object.

Einstein went on to develop the General Theory of Relativity
with the aim of explaining gravitation. According to the
General Theory, any mass tends to distort or "bend" space
itself. The larger the mass, the greater the bending, so the
distortion of space around a very large mass like a planet is
considerable. As a result of such distortion, bodies tend to
move towards each other in precisely the way bodies are
attracted to each other by gravity. The General Theory demonstrated that gravity was a property of the "shape" of space
itself.

This theory led to some surprising predictions. According to
Einstein's reasoning, light rays ought to bend slightly as they
pass close to a large mass like the sun. Many scientists
dismissed this idea as absurd. Then in 1919 a total eclipse of
the sun made it possible to measure light rays passing close to it
from distant stars. It was discovered that light did bend in the
sun's gravitational field.

Einstein saw space and time as being somehow bound
together into a unity called space-time. If we were able to
step outside our Universe and look in, we might see the
Universe as a gigantic ball of space-time. Moreover, we would

notice that it was more curved in the region of any large mass like a star or a planet.

The Theory of Relativity is extremely complex, and can only be fully understood with the aid of mathematical formulas. However, what matters from our point of view is that scientific research strongly suggests that the theory is correct, and that the space and time which we take for granted are far stranger than we think. A striking illustration of this is the recently advanced theory of so-called "black holes". This holds that certain stars burned themselves out like giant atom bombs, collapsed in on themselves, and became ever smaller and denser. Afterwards their gravitational fields got stronger. It is possible that the pressures exerted by a collapsing star could be so tremendous that it would go on collapsing forever, forming a black hole in space. The gravitational field would be so strong that not even light could escape from it. Anything that fell into a black hole would never get out again – any spaceship or planet that got sucked into this whirlpool of destruction could never escape.

Ideas like these fail to make sense in terms of the world we see around us. Yet there are certain spots on the surface of our Earth where we may be able to gain some impression of the strange effects of space-time. For example, on the banks of Sardine Creek, Oregon, there is a spot known as the "Oregon Vortex". It is about 165 feet across, and the force of gravity seems to be intensified towards its centre. Compasses and other instruments refuse to work in the vortex, and a photographer's light meter reveals a considerable difference in intensity between the daylight in the circle and that outside. There is a hut in the vortex – an old office abandoned long ago. It has slipped downhill, and is now at a slight angle towards the centre of the circle. People who step into the hut experience a weird sense of unbalance, as if they were in a hall of distorted mirrors at a fairground. This feeling is not entirely an illusion. A ball dangling from a beam in the ceiling of the hut seems to incline toward the centre of the vortex. Observations made from outside the vortex prove that this is so. Visitors feel pulled toward the centre of the circle, and seem compelled to lean backward at an angle. Cigarette smoke in the vortex spirals upward in a strange manner, and a handful of confetti whirls around as if caught in a twister.

It has been suggested that the phenomena of the vortex are due to electromagnetism, but they could equally be the man-

ifestation of some eccentricity in the laws of gravity. Add to this
the idea that "waves" of space-time are not fixed, but roll across
the universe in a definite rhythm, and we begin to see how
certain spots could be freakish and unpredictable. We cannot
understand much about their mechanism, but we can see that
such a space-time warp could have strange consequences for
anyone who happened to get caught in it. Like Orion Williamson, who disappeared in full view of two friends. Like the
Spanish soldier who was teleported from the Philippines to
Mexico City. Or like Benjamin Bathurst, the British Ambassa-
dor to the court of Francis I of Austria, who, in the presence of
his secretary and valet, strolled around the post horses that
were to carry him back to London, and simply vanished. This
happened on 25 November 1809 – and Bathurst was never seen
again. The British suspected that their arch-enemy Napoleon
was behind the disappearance, but Napoleon flatly denied
knowing anything about it. He might have pointed out that
even his secret police had no power to make a man vanish into
thin air in front of two witnesses.

Charles Fort mentions the Benjamin Bathurst case, among
many other strange disappearances, but has no explanation to
suggest. In fact, the space-time warp idea might explain many
of the strange phenomena recorded by Fort: the fish, frogs, coal,
sand, and rain of blood that have fallen out of clear skies onto
the earth. If a space-time warp could transport a Spanish
soldier 9000 miles, it might just as easily transport fish from
the depths of the sea to the midwestern plains of North
America.

Fort mentions in passing a detail that modern researchers
may find highly significant: the strange events he records are
often accompanied by a failure of electric power in machines.
Such an inexplicable power failure occurred in Cairo on 5 April
1923. It is linked by some with the famous "curse of Tutankhamun" because it coincided with the death of the Earl of
Carnarvon, the man who sponsored the excavation of Tutankhamun's tomb. The same thing happened in Denver, Color-
ado, on 14 February 1963: all power failed, and engineers found
the failure inexplicable. They were equally baffled when the
lights came on again an hour and a half later. Flying saucer
enthusiasts point out that similar failures seem to occur in the
vicinity of UFOs. For example, on 17 August 1959 the Chief
Engineer of the power station in Uberlandia, Minais Gerais,
Brazil, saw a large flying object passing over the station. At the

same moment, the automatic power switches kicked themselves open. The engineer closed them; they flew open again. The flying object passed over a substation a few miles away, and the keys there flew open in the same way. While the UFO hovered near the station, the keys refused to remain closed. When it flew off, everything functioned normally again.

Ufologists are inclined to believe that the motors of a UFO cause power failures. As far as I know, no one has yet suggested the more interesting hypothesis that UFOs may be associated with space-time warps, and that it is the warp that is to blame.

As the British scientist J.B.S. Haldane once remarked: ''The universe is not only stranger than we imagine; it is stranger than we *can* imagine.''

chapter four

DEVIL'S GRAVEYARDS

*I*t is odd that we should call our planet the Earth. It would be far more reasonable to call it the Sea. Almost three quarters of this globe is under water, and if the polar caps melted, about half the remaining land would vanish. We human beings are little better than shipwrecked sailors living on tiny islands. The Pacific Ocean alone is larger than all the land areas of the world, and it is so deep that it could contain the whole landmass of the moon.

Because we have sailed all over the sea's surface, we believe that we know the sea. This is a fallacy. A mere two per cent of the ocean's floor has been charted. At its greatest depth, the Pacific Ocean is seven miles deep. As undersea explorer Jacques Cousteau has remarked, the sea is like a bowl of soup, and it gets thicker as you get deeper. It used to be thought that no life could exist at such a depth, but special deep-sea submarines – one of which reached a depth of almost seven miles – have revealed that this is an error. New marine species are always being discovered. In 1938 a fisherman in the Indian Ocean caught a coelacanth, a prehistoric fish that was believed to have died out sixty million years ago. There are reasonable grounds for believing that 100-foot long eels still exist in the ocean. The oceanographer Alain Bombard, making a one-man trip across the Atlantic in a rubber dinghy, was followed by an unknown sea creature he described as "a long, green sausage, about ten feet long and nine inches or so in diameter. It was not seaweed because it moved and wriggled . . ." The more we learn of the sea, the more obvious it becomes that we have scarcely begun to penetrate its mysteries.

To human beings the most frightening characteristic of the sea is its power to engulf them without trace. I am not speaking of straightforward drowning – the sea has a habit of yielding up its drowned – but of the strange disappearances at sea that are even more numerous and more baffling than those on land.

One of the more curious of the sea's minor enigmas is the mystery of the Eilean Mor lighthouse on the Flannan Islands off the west coast of Scotland. Ten days before Christmas in 1900, the lighthouse's 140,000 candlepower light was extinguished. Joseph Moore, the relief lighthouse keeper in the Outer Hebrides seventeen miles away, could not leave his post to investigate because wild storms of the North Atlantic had battered the coast for a week past.

Among the inhabitants of the Hebrides the Flannan Islands have the reputation of being haunted. Eilean Mor, the largest of the islands, has a fine green turf that is highly suitable for sheep, and farmers would sometimes take their sheep there for fattening. But nothing would persuade them to remain on the island overnight.

On 26 December the storm abated, and the steamer *Hesperus* set out for Eilean Mor with provisions. As the *Hesperus* circled the island, the crew observed that no preparations had been made for their arrival. There were no empty packing cases or mooring ropes on the jetty. A boat was let down, and Joseph Moore was the first ashore. The entrance gate and the main door of the lighthouse were closed. Moore went inside and shouted. There was no reply. The place was cold and empty. The clock on the shelf had stopped. Moore ran back to the jetty for help, afraid that he might find dead men in the lighthouse turret. Two men climbed the stairs with him. But there was no sign of life. The entire lighthouse was empty. In the sleeping quarters the beds were made, and everything was neat and orderly. The wicks of the lanterns had been trimmed, and they had been filled with oil ready to be lit after dark. The last entry on the record slate had been made at 9 a.m. on 15 December – the day the light had failed to appear.

At first it looked as if the mystery might be solved. Two of the three sets of oilskins belonging to the lighthouse keepers were missing. Investigators who landed on the island a few days later found that the west jetty had suffered severe storm

Early deep sea exploration vessel, the French Bathyscape reached depths of 4050 metres in 1954

damage. On a concrete platform sixty-five feet above the water stood a crane with ropes trailing from it. These ropes were usually kept in a tool chest, which was placed in a crevice more than a hundred feet above sea level. The chest was found to be missing. The astonishing conclusion was that some tremendous storm, with waves over a hundred feet high, seemed to have battered the island and carried away the chest – draping its ropes over the crane – and swept the three men to their deaths.

For that to have happened was well nigh impossible. To begin with, the day of the 15th had been relatively calm despite a week of storms. If this were not the case, all three oilskins would have been missing, whereas one had been left behind in the lighthouse. Furthermore, experienced lighthouse men would hardly be stupid enough to venture out onto a jetty in a storm.

It seems far more likely that the damage to the jetty had occurred in a storm the previous evening, and that the three men had gone out in calm weather to inspect it. And then what happened? One suggestion that gained wide general acceptance is that one of the three went insane, killed his two companions, and then committed suicide. But no weapons were missing. Hammers, axes, and knives were all untouched in their proper places.

Three men had set out for the west jetty of their lighthouse on a calm day – and vanished. No bodies were ever recovered. No plausible explanation has ever been put forward. Moore, left alone in the lighthouse for two days after landing, believed that he heard men's voices calling to him. Could they have been other than the cry of sea birds? Since 1900 no more disappearances have occurred, and the island has kept its secret.

As we examine some of the classic mysteries of the sea, a pattern begins to emerge. In case after case something frightened the crew into abandoning ship. No one has ever been able to suggest what that something might be.

The case of the Dutch schooner *Hermania* is typical. In 1849 a fishing vessel off the coast of Cornwall in southwest England found the ship drifting. She had been dismasted, evidently by a gale. Men went aboard and found that the schooner's lifeboat was still in its chocks. The property of the crew seemed to be intact, but every living soul aboard the vessel had vanished.

An even stranger mystery was encountered by another British sailing vessel, the *Ellen Austin*. In the summer of 1881 the ship was heading for St John's, Newfoundland. In the mid-

Atlantic, the crew sighted a schooner that seemed to be keeping a parallel course. As they came closer they realized that the ship was drifting. A boarding party examined the schooner. Everything seemed to be in order, and there was no sign of a struggle; but the crew was missing. The mate and several crew members from the *Ellen Austin* stayed on board to man the valuable prize, and for some time the two ships continued to sail parallel. Then a storm blew up, driving them apart. When the storm had cleared, the mystery ship seemed to be damaged. The captain saw through his telescope that there was no one on deck. He ordered a boat to be lowered, and went on board. The ship was deserted.

His crew went into a panic. It took the captain a great deal of talking – with offers of reward – to persuade a four-man crew to go aboard the derelict. Again, the two ships proceeded toward Newfoundland. The mystery schooner was faster than the *Ellen Austin*, and soon drew ahead. That didn't bother the captain, however, because he expected to find the ship in St John's when he arrived. But there was no sign of the schooner in port. It had vanished with the crew members.

In October 1917 the schooner *Zebrina* left Falmouth, England, for France – a fairly short voyage. Two days later, the *Zebrina* was found drifting and deserted with no sign of violence or anything else to indicate why the crew had left. In July 1941 the Portuguese lugger *Islandia* sighted the French cutter *Belle Isle* near the Gulf of Lyon. The sails of the cutter were set and undamaged. There was no one aboard, and no clue to the disappearance of the sailors was found. All these cases seem to have the same strange element in common – the mysterious something that caused panic, and left no clue behind.

The chief problem in most of these cases is lack of adequate documentation, which leads the critical reader to suspect the accuracy of most popular accounts. In at least two classic cases, however, we have accurate and detailed documentation. These are the mysteries of the *Mary Celeste* and the *Joyita*.

From the beginning, the American vessel *Mary Celeste* was an unlucky ship. Her first captain died a few days after taking command. On her first voyage she damaged her hull. In the Straits of Dover she collided with a brig and sank it. In 1867, only six years after her launching, she grounded on Cape Breton Island, Nova Scotia, and was assumed to be a write-off. A man who salvaged her went bankrupt.

In the autumn of 1872, with this history behind her, the *Mary*

Celeste set out from New York with a cargo of commercial alcohol. Captain Benjamin Briggs had his wife and two-year-old daughter on board, and there was a crew of seven. The *Mary Celeste* sailed for the Italian port of Genoa on 5 November. Ten days later, the British ship *Dei Gratia* also left New York bound for Gibraltar. Her captain was David Moorhouse.

On the afternoon of 5 December 1872 the *Dei Gratia* sighted the *Mary Celeste* in the North Atlantic, midway between the Azores and the coast of Portugal. She was obviously drifting. A boarding party found her deserted. The lifeboat was missing, indicating that the crew had abandoned ship in some kind of danger. But there was nothing noticeably wrong with the vessel. There were a few feet of water in the hold, but the ship's pumps proved to be working perfectly, and this was soon pumped out. The condition of the crew's quarters indicated that the ship had been abandoned in extreme haste. In the hold a few barrels of the commercial alcohol had broken open, and one was empty. The hatch of the hold was found on deck.

With some difficulty a skeleton crew sailed the *Mary Celeste*

In November 1964 Chuck Wakely, a pilot for a charter flight airline, had a narrow escape from being swallowed up by the unknown forces of the Bermuda Triangle. At the time of his frightening experience, he knew nothing about the perils of that area.

Wakely's brush with fate occurred on a return solo flight from Nassau to Miami. He climbed to 8000 feet, levelled off, and settled back for a routine run. Then he noticed a faint glow on the wings of his plane. He put it down to an optical illusion created by the cockpit lights through the tinted windows.

After about five minutes, however, the glow increased so much that Wakely found it hard to read his instruments. Soon he had to operate the craft manually because none of the electronic equipment was in working order.

He noticed that the wings glowed bluish-green and looked fuzzy. At that point he was in such operating difficulties that he had to let go of the controls and let the plane take its head. The glow became blinding, but then began to fade.

As soon as the glow had died down, the instruments began to work properly again. Wakely was able to make a normal landing at his destination.

He was one of the lucky ones.

to Gibraltar, arriving on 13 December. Right from the start they met with hostility. The British authorities in Gibraltar suspected that the men of the *Dei Gratia* were in collusion with the crew of the *Mary Celeste* to claim salvage money. The *Mary Celeste* was searched, and on 18 December an inquiry was heard in the Vice-Admiralty Court of Gibraltar. The Queen's Advocate, Solly Flood, who cross-examined the witnesses, concluded that there had been a mutiny aboard the *Mary Celeste*, and that the crew had killed the captain and his family. Searchers had found a cutlass under the captain's bed, and Flood maintained that certain stains on it were blood. The hull of the ship appeared to have been damaged, and Flood believed that the mutineers did this to make it look as if the vessel had struck rocks. The United States consul in Gibraltar disagreed hotly with this view. He insisted that there were no signs whatever of violence or mutiny aboard the *Mary Celeste*, and that the damage to the hull was natural.

The crew of the *Dei Gratia* was finally awarded £1700 salvage money – a mere fraction of the ship's value. And so the whole incident was forgotten – for eleven years. At that time an impecunious young doctor with ambitions to become an author wrote a story based on the affair. Entitled "*J. Habakuk Jephson's Statement*," the story appeared anonymously in *The Cornhill Magazine* in January 1884 with the ship's name changed to *Marie Celeste*. The story claimed that she had been taken over as part of what would now be called a Black Power plot. It also claimed that the vessel's lifeboat was still on board when she was found. When the identity of the author became known, he found himself launched on the road to fame.

The author was Arthur Conan Doyle, and his fictional version of the *Mary Celeste* mystery started a flood of books and articles on the subject. Most of them were speculation or pure fiction, and none of these accounts succeeded in throwing any light on the reasons for the ship's abandonment. One of the few plausible suggestions is that some of the alcohol on board exploded – which could account for the hatch being on the deck – and the captain decided that they should all climb into one lifeboat to be towed behind the *Mary Celeste*. At some point, the tow broke and everyone drowned. The only objection to this explanation is that there was no sign of an explosion in the hold.

The *Joyita* is often referred to as the *Mary Celeste* of the Pacific. It was a twin-screw ship that met with disaster in October 1955 some time after leaving Apia in Western Samoa. It was headed for Fakaofo in the Tokelau Islands, a mere 270 miles to the north. On 10 November, more than a month after she had set out, the *Joyita* was found abandoned and half foundering. But the ship was cork-lined, and therefore practically unsinkable. The captain, Dusty Miller, had known that perfectly well – in fact, he had often boasted of it. His officers knew it too. So why had they abandoned ship?

Stranger still, there were signs that two men had stayed aboard. An awning had been erected either to catch water or to keep off the sun. Where had these men gone?

There could be no doubt whatever that the *Joyita* had been in trouble. In fact, only one of the two engines was working, and the radio was defective. She was hardly seaworthy.

The ship was taken to Suva, Fiji, where she was dry-docked and pumped out. The basic cause of the trouble was soon apparent. A pipe under the boiler room floor had broken and flooded the vessel. Blood-stained bandages were found. This suggested that someone had been injured fairly seriously – probably the captain himself, since he would otherwise not have permitted the crew to abandon ship. It therefore seemed possible to reconstruct the tragedy. Somewhere out at sea, the *Joyita*'s engine stopped. The pipe burst and caused flooding. Captain Miller had somehow been badly injured, perhaps by being thrown from the bridge by a sudden listing. The crew and passengers had taken to the boats, and had perished at sea. Miller had remained on board, probably with a devoted attendant to look after him.

And then . . . what? At this point, we once again meet with a mystery. Did some new panic cause the captain and his companion to abandon ship? That is unlikely, since Miller knew that his ship was unsinkable. Even if the captain had died of his wound and was thrown overboard, surely his companion would have remained. One theory is that the drifting vessel encountered a pirate ship, and that Miller and his companion were murdered. It is true that some of the cargo was missing; but it seems likely that this was thrown overboard in the original panic to lighten the ship. In the two decades since it met disaster, the *Joyita* has joined the *Mary Celeste* as one of the unsolved mysteries of the sea. At this stage, it seems unlikely that the truth will ever come to light.

The cases described so far have occurred in many different parts of the world, but there are two small areas that have been

As a British steamer plowed its way through the Persian Gulf near Oman in the summer of 1906, an enormous wheel of light appeared. The vast wheel, seemingly bigger than the ship itself, was revolving in the sky not far above the surface of the water at that point. Vivid shafts of light emitted from the huge wheel and passed right through the steamer. But these beams fortunately did not interfere with the functioning of the boat in any way.

Since 1760 seamen have recounted sightings of unidentified flying objects in the form of a wheel. The Persian Gulfsighting of 1906 was one of eleven recorded reports between 1848 and 1910. Like most of the sea accounts of mysterious luminous wheels, this one remarked on the eery silence of the phenomenon. Also in common with most other such reports, nothing was said about humans or human-like beings in the wheels, even though the ascent and descent of these objects were obviously controlled.

Were such glowing wheels in the sky an early and less sophisticated form of flying saucer? Were they operated by beings from other planets who kept themselves hidden or were invisible? Were they just visions of mariners too long at sea? No one has found an answer.

responsible for more disappearances than the rest of the world put together. They are know as the "Bermuda Triangle" and the "Devil's Sea". One lies in the Atlantic off the east coast of the United States, the other in the Pacific south-east of Japan. Both have acquired a singularly evil reputation.

The term "Bermuda Triangle" was coined by the author of a book on sea mysteries, Vincent Gaddis, who also called it the "Triangle of Death". Gaddis was among the first to notice the incredible number of disappearances of ships and aircraft in this relatively small area off the coast of Florida. Well over a hundred such disappearances have been recorded, with the loss of more than a thousand lives. Most of these mysteries have occurred since 1945, and the disappearances have been total. Not a single body nor a fragment of wreckage from the vanished craft has ever been recovered.

A typical disappearance took place on 8 January 1962. A big United States Air Force Boeing Stratotanker took off from Langley, Virginia, and flew east for the Azores. Shortly afterwards the control tower received weak radio signals from the plane. When these ceased, the wide-scale search was launched. But no trace of the aircraft was ever found.

The long saga of disappearances in the Triangle begins in the year 1609. A ship called the *Sea Venture*, bearing English settlers to Virginia, was shipwrecked off the island of Bermuda. On 1 September the longboat of the wrecked vessel set out on the 500-mile voyage to the coast of the United States to bring help. With a fair wind in its sail, it passed beyond the horizon – and was never seen again.

In 1750 five Spanish treasure ships were caught in storms off Cape Hatteras. Three of them vanished completely, and no wreckage was found.

In 1800 two United States Navy ships vanished in the area. In his book on the Bermuda Triangle, Charles Berlitz lists twelve more cases of major vessels that have disappeared in the Triangle, and no less than seven cases of ships found drifting, like the *Mary Celeste*, abandoned but basically undamaged. His list begins with the *Rosalie*, a large French vessel found abandoned in 1840 with sails set and cargo intact, and ends with the total disappearance on 23 March 1973 of the 20,000-ton freighter *Anita*.

The disappearance of planes in the Triangle area began on 5 December 1945, when five United States Navy aircraft vanished on a routine training flight. Each plane should have been manned by an officer pilot and two crew members, but one of the crew members had a premonition of disaster and stayed away. The planes were Avenger torpedo bombers, and each had enough fuel for more than a thousand miles. Their projected flight was less than 500 miles. They took off from their base at Fort Lauderdale, Florida, at 2 p.m. At about 3.15 p.m., the control tower received a strange message from the flight leader. He reported that the planes seemed to be off course, and he could not see land. Asked to state his position, he said he didn't know. Clearly the aircrafts' compasses and navigation gear were not functioning. This was confirmed shortly afterward when control overheard conversations between the planes in which crew members referred to the instruments in all the planes as "going crazy". Each registered a different reading, they said. Meanwhile, heavy static had begun to obscure communications. The planes seemed unable to hear the base transmitter, and it became increasingly difficult for control to hear them. The last barely audible message from the planes was received at 4 p.m. It said again that the pilots could not be sure where they were.

Rescue planes were dispatched among which was a twin-engined Martin Mariner with a crew of thirteen. Shortly after takeoff, base also lost contact with the Martin Mariner. Like the five planes it sought, it was never heard from again. In spite of an intensive search involving over 300 planes and many hundreds of sailing vessels, no trace of the six missing aircraft was ever found.

In his book Charles Berlitz lists fourteen more planes that have disappeared in the Triangle area since 1945. In case after case, the same phrase recurs: "lost radio contact".

Berlitz was by no means the first person to write about the Bermuda Triangle, but he was the first to investigate reports of people who had narrowly escaped its strange perils. Captain Don Henry, owner of a salvage company in Florida, described how, in 1966, he was aboard a tug towing an empty petroleum-nitrate barge. The weather was clear and calm. Suddenly the tug's compass began to spin clockwise. The sea became turbulent. "We couldn't see where the horizon was – the water, sky, and horizon all blended together," Captain Henry recalled. All electrical appliances stopped working. The generators continued to run, but there was no electricity. The barge had vanished beneath a cloud of fog. Henry signalled full speed ahead, but had the feeling that something was holding them back. Then suddenly the tug pulled free. For a few minutes the barge remained hidden in a dense fog – although there was no fog anywhere else – but the tug gradually towed it out. The tug's generators began to work normally again, but all the batteries were dead, and several flashlight batteries had to be thrown away.

In April 1963 the crew of a Boeing 707 observed what looked like an atomic explosion in the sea. They saw the water rise up into a great mound, half a mile wide. The pilot later checked with the coast guard and meteorological agencies to find out if there had been an earthquake in the area, but he was told that no unusual occurrences had been reported.

The baffling element in most of these accounts is not the strange behavior of the compasses, but the loss of electric power. Compasses behave strangely if brought close to a large magnet or mass of iron ore, and there could well be some vast iron deposit under the seabed in the Triangle area. But there is no way known to science of draining a battery of its charge, or preventing a generator from producing electricity – if there were, it would be an invaluable weapon of war. Yet the force that operates in the area of the Bermuda Triangle seems to interfere with electrical circuits.

The evidence about sea disappearances, like those on land, appears to tie in with the notion of some disturbance of the gravitational field – an "antigravity warp" – in which the laws of gravity do not operate in conventional ways. However, such speculation only serves to emphasize how little we really know about gravity, and that we have no way of judging how it might be affected by local conditions. All we can say is that, *if* there is such a thing as an antigravity warp, the local conditions in the Bermuda Triangle would certainly appear to be an example of it.

The same observation may well apply to the "Devil's Sea" – an area in the Pacific 800 miles south-east of Japan between Iwo Jima and Marcus Island. Perhaps because this area is so far from the coast of Japan, its mysteries have never aroused the same excitement as those of the Bermuda Triangle. There had been occasional disappearances of ships and aircraft in the area over a long period; but between 1950 and 1954 no less than nine ships disappeared without trace. The Japanese government then became concerned, and declared it a danger zone. In 1955 the government sponsored an expedition to the area, and a group of scientists set sail aboard the *Kaiyo Maru No. 5*. The *Kaiyo Maru* itself vanished.

Ivan T. Sanderson, an avid collector of strange incidents, tried marking the Bermuda Triangle and the Devil's Sea on a map. He observed that the two areas lie in roughly the same latitude – between 30 and 40 north of the Equator – and are approximately the same size. Other observations of areas known as "devil's graveyards" led Sanderson to conclude that there are twelve such zones lying symmetrically around the world. Two of these are the North and South poles. Others lie neatly at intervals of 72 around the globe, and are centered at 36 north and south latitudes. Sanderson suggests that the Bermuda Triangle is the most notorious because it happens to be one of the busiest areas of the world. Apart from the Poles, only two of the devil's graveyards lie on land – one in the area of the Sahara desert, the other in the mountainous region of north-western India.

Sanderson noted that most of the suspect areas lie in parts of the ocean where warm and cold currents collide, and that these

areas are "nodal points" where surface and subsurface currents
turn in different directions. His suggestion is that the powerful
sweeping movement of subsurface tidal currents, influenced by
variations in temperature, causes magnetic vortices that are the
root of the trouble. There is no evidence, however, that the
collision of ocean currents produces changes in the earth's
magnetism. There is no reason why it should. Nor does
Sanderson's theory apply to the land areas – the Sahara,
northern India, the Poles. If "magnetic vortices" provide the
answer isn't it more likely that these are nodal points in the
earth's field of power?

It must be acknowledged that Sanderson has provided the
basis for an interesting theory. Even his suggestion, however,
fails to explain why so many ships have been found abandoned, with no clue as to what caused the crew to leave in
panic.

chapter five

THE MAN WHO STUDIED GHOULS

*T*he nearest British equivalent of Charles Fort was a retired Cambridge don named T.C. Lethbridge, known to his friends as Tom. When he died in a Devon nursing home in 1971, his name was hardly known to the British public. Today, many of his admirers believe he was the single most important name in paranormal research. But unlike Fort, who was contented to collect weird phenomena in an attempt to confound scientists, Lethbridge's whole life was an attempt to understand "the unexplained".

Lethbridge was trained as an archaeologist and historian, and spent most of his adult life as the Keeper of Anglo-Saxon Antiquities at the University Museum in Cambridge. But even in this respectable setting, he was always upsetting his colleagues. They were particularly shocked at the rumour that he used a dowsing-rod or a pendulum to try to locate objects buried underground. Finally, he left Cambridge in disgust at the hostile reception of one of his books on archaeology. Together with his wife Mina, he moved into Hole House, an old Tudor mansion on the south coast of Devon. He meant to spend his retirement reading and digging for bits of broken pottery. In fact, the most amazing period of his eventful life was about to begin.

The person who was most responsible for this change of direction was an old "witch" who lived next door. This white-haired little old lady assured Lethbridge that she could put

mild spells on people who annoyed her, and that she was able
to leave her body at night and wander around the district – an
ability known as "astral projection". Lethbridge was naturally
sceptical – until something convinced him.

The witch explained to him one day how she managed to put
off unwanted visitors. What she did was to draw a five pointed
star – a pentagram – in her head, and then visualise it across the
path of the unwanted visitor – for example, on the front gate.

Shortly afterwards, Tom was lying in bed, idly drawing
pentagrams in his head, and imagining them around their
beds. In the middle of the night, Mina woke up with a creepy
feeling that there was somebody else in the room. At the foot of
the bed, she could see a faint glow of light, which slowly faded
as she watched it. The next day, the witch came to see them.
When she told them that she had "visited" their bedroom on
the previous night, and found the beds surrounded by triangles
of fire, Tom's scepticism began to evaporate. Mina politely
requested the old witch to stay out of their bedroom at night.

Three years later, the old lady died in peculiar circumstances.
She was quarrelling with a neighbouring farmer, and told
Lethbridge that she intended to put a spell on the man's
cattle. By this time, Lethbridge knew enough about the
"occult" to take her seriously, and he warned her about the
dangers of black magic – how it could rebound on to the witch.
But the old lady ignored his advice. One morning, she was
found dead in her bed in circumstances that made the police
suspect murder. And the cattle of two nearby farms suddenly
got foot and mouth disease. However, the farmer she wanted to
"ill wish" remained unaffected. Lethbridge was convinced that
the spell had gone wrong and "bounced back".

But the old lady's death resulted – indirectly – in one of his
most important insights. Passing the witch's cottage, he experienced a "nasty feeling", a suffocating sense of depression.
With a scientist's curiosity, he walked around the cottage, and
noticed an interesting thing. He could step *into* the depression
and then out of it again, just as if it was some kind of invisible
wall.

The depression reminded Lethbridge of something that had
happened when he was a teenager. He and his mother had
gone for a walk in the Great Wood near Wokingham. It was a
lovely morning; yet quite suddenly, both of them experienced
"a horrible feeling of gloom and depression, which crept upon
us like a blanket of fog over the surface of the sea". They

The altar in most Christian churches is placed at the east end of the building. This is a tradition based on the idea that facing the direction of the sunrise symbolizes turning toward spiritual light.

This tradition, oddly enough, may account for the fact that the nave and chancel of many of the old churches in Great Britain lie at an angle to each other rather than in a straight line. In Oxfordshire alone, for example, there are eighty-one churches with crooked chancels (the part of the building housing the altar). Why were these and many other chancels throughout the rest of the country built at an angle?

The Reverend Hugh Benson of Plymouth, England, thinks it is because the churches were meant to face sunrise on the exact festival day of their particular patron saint.

According to his letter-to-the-editor of *The Times* of London in 1975, Reverend Benson has studied this matter over a period of years, and has examined nearly a thousand churches. After making careful calculations, he became convinced that a great many churches had in fact faced sunrise on their saint's day at the time they were built. There were only about half a dozen exceptions to this finding in the whole of his survey.

"Now it follows," he says, "that a church built in honor of St Mary, for example, and facing sunrise on 25 March, would after a century or so, owing to the Julian calendar, be found to be facing too far south. If then a new chancel was built, it would be set out to face the new sunrise position . . . The crookedness of the chancel, far from being due to carelessness, is due to a most scrupulous care."

hurried away, agreeing that it was something terrible and inexplicable. A few days later, the corpse of a suicide was found a few yards from the spot where they had been standing, hidden by some bushes.

About a year after the death of the witch, another strange experience gave Tom the clue he was looking for. On a damp January afternoon, he and Mina drove down to Ladram Bay to collect seaweed for her garden. As Lethbridge stepped on to the beach, he once again experienced the feeling of gloom and fear, like a blanket of fog descending upon him. Mina wandered off along the beach while Tom filled the sacks with seaweed. Suddenly she came hurrying back, saying: "Let's go. I can't stand this place a minute longer. There's something frightful here."

The next day, they mentioned what had happened to Mina's brother. He said he also had experienced the same kind of thing in a field near Avebury, in Wiltshire. The word "field" made something connect in Tom's brain – he remembered that field telephones often short-circuit in warm, muggy weather. "What was the weather like?" he asked. "Warm and damp," said the brother.

An idea was taking shape. *Water* . . . could that be the key? It had been warm and damp in the Great Wood. It had been warm and damp on Ladram beach. The following weekend, they set out for Ladram Bay a second time. Again, as they stepped on to the beach, both walked into the same bank of depression – or "ghoul" as Lethbridge called it. Mina led Tom to the far end of the beach, to the place she had been sitting when she had been overwhelmed by the strange feeling. Here it was so strong that it made them feel giddy – Lethbridge described it as the feeling you get when you have a high temperature and are full of drugs. On either side of them were two small streams.

Mina wandered off to look at the scenery from the top of the cliff. Suddenly, she walked into the depression again. Moreover, she had an odd feeling, as if someone – or something – was urging her to jump over. She went and fetched Tom, who agreed that the spot was just as sinister as the place down on the seashore below.

Now he needed only one more piece of the jigsaw puzzle, and he found it – but only years later. 'Nine years before Tom and Mina's experience of depression on those cliffs, a man had committed suicide there. Lethbridge wondered whether the "ghoul" was a feeling so intense that it had become timeless and imprinted itself on the area, casting its baleful shadow on those who stood there.

Whether from the past or from the future the feelings of despair were "recorded" on the surroundings – but how?

The key, Lethbridge believed, was water. As an archaeologist, he had always been mildly interested in dowsing and water-divining. The dowser walks along with a forked hazel twig held in his hands, and when he stands above running water, the muscles in his hands and arms convulse and the twig bends either up or down. How does it work? Professor Y. Rocard of the Sorbonne discovered that underground water produces changes in the earth's magnetic field, and this is what the dowser's muscles respond to. The water does this

'King Faria' of San Rafael, California, a water witch

because it has a field of its own, which interacts with the earth's field.

Significantly, magnetic fields are the means by which sound is recorded on tape covered with iron oxide. Suppose the magnetic field of running water can also record strong emotions – which, after all, are basically electrical activities in the human brain and body? Such fields could well be strongest in damp and muggy weather.

This would also explain why the banks of depression seem to form a kind of invisible wall. Anyone who has ever tried bringing a magnet closer and closer to an iron nail will know that the nail is suddenly "seized" by the magnet as it enters the force field. Presumably the magnetic field of water has the same property. And if it can "tape record" powerful emotions, then you would feel them quite suddenly, as you stepped into the field. Both Tom and Mina noticed that the ghoul on Ladram beach came to an end quite abruptly.

What fascinated Lethbridge so much was that he was beginning to discover *scientific* reasons for events that are generally labelled "supernatural". If the gloom of a suicide can "record" itself on the electrical field of water, would a dowsing rod provide more information about the nature of the field? In fact, many dowsers prefer a pendulum to a dowsing rod, believing that it is more sensitive. Now that Lethbridge had embarked on this weird study of witches and electrical fields, he decided to give it a try. He started by carving a one inch ball out of a piece of hazel wood, and threading it on a long piece of string, which he wound around a pencil. Next, he placed a silver dish on the floor, and held his pendulum over it. Then he carefully unwound the string. When it reached a length of exactly twenty-two inches, the pendulum stopped swinging back and forth, and began to go round in a circle. Lethbridge concluded that a pendulum of exactly twenty-two inches "reacts" to silver. Next, he tried it over a copper pot; this time it reacted at thirty and a half inches. He spent the rest of the day testing different substances to discover their "rates": sulphur, aluminium, gold, diamond, sand. He even tried holding the pendulum over organic substances like milk, oranges and apples. In each case, it reacted quite exactly at a definite length.

For his next experiment, he went out into the courtyard of his home – part of which had been built in the fourteenth century – and walked around slowly, holding the pendulum by its string.

After a short time, the back-and-forth swing of the pendulum changed to a circular motion. Lethbridge took a spade, and proceeded to dig cautiously at the point the motion had changed. Just under the turf he found a piece of seventeenth-century pottery, and six inches lower a piece of seventeenth-century Rhineland stoneware. But this was not what he was looking for. Twenty-two inches is the length at which the pendulum should be able to locate silver. Lethbridge held his pendulum over the heap of earth from the hole. It swung in a circle. He searched carefully through the heap of earth, but failed to find the expected silver. Finally, as he was filling the hole, he found another piece of old stoneware. He held the pendulum over it, and the pendulum swung with a violent circular movement. Then he remembered: old stoneware is glazed with lead salts, and lead is on the same "wavelength" as silver. The mystery was explained.

Any reader who is inclined to dismiss this as a typical crank theory should first of all try dowsing – an art that is thousands of years old. Take any kind of bead or bob and thread it on the end of a long piece of string. Now take a ruler, and measure off precisely twenty-four inches on the string. Ask any male of your acquaintance to lie down on the floor, and hold the pendulum over him. Start the pendulum swinging gently to and fro. After a few moments, this arc swing will change to a circular motion. If you hold the pendulum over a female, nothing will happen – the pendulum will continue to swing back and forth. However, if you increase the length of the string to twenty-nine inches, the pendulum will react over women, and will show no reaction for men. This is because twenty-nine inches is the so-called "female length". According to diviners, each substance has its own wavelength. Twenty-four inches will locate diamonds and males. Twenty-nine inches will locate gold, females, and anything colored yellow.

The behavior of a ball on the end of a piece of string may seem a far cry from the mysterious electrical or magnetic fields that can cause a ship's compass to spin wildly. However, it is significant that dowsers have insisted on the existence of such fields for centuries. Indeed, the dowser's ability to locate water, minerals, and other substances underground may be due to picking up the activity of these fields.

Lethbridge tells an interesting story about visiting an ancient stone circle called the Merry Maidens near Penzance, Cornwall.

This circle is believed to date from the same time as Stonehenge, about 1500 BC. Presumably it served some religious purpose, but nobody knows which. Lethbridge tried his pendulum close to one of the stones, setting it at thirty inches. This is the length that diviners use for testing the age of ancient monuments. As he held the pendulum, Lethbridge rested his free hand on the stone megalith. Almost as soon as the pendulum started to swing, the hand resting on the stone received a tingling sensation like an electric shock, and the pendulum began to circle so strongly that it was almost horizontal. Some very powerful force was apparently at work.

I have myself experienced the mysterious force at the Merry Maidens when dowsing with a friend who is interested in the subject. Although I had only tried dowsing once before – without success – on this occasion I obtained a powerful reaction. I was using a dowsing rod made of two thin springy strips of whalebone tied together at one end. As I walked toward the centre of the stone circle, holding the rod as directed by my friend, the rod began to push upward until

---

Experiments with dowsing led the British ethnologist T. C. Lethbridge to believe strongly in magnetic fields, or fields of force, as a possible explanation of ghosts. He tells this story about one ghost he saw.

According to Lethbridge, he was standing on a hill above a mill. A little stream ran nearby, vanishing into the slope of the hill. Below him, about 60 yards away, a woman stood near the mill. Her clothes were about forty years out of date. On investigation he discovered that no one remotely resembling the woman he had seen had been near the mill at the time. He had seen a ghost.

Lethbridge explained this by his field-of-force theory. Someone, he said, had once been on the hill, and had seen the figure he had seen. The sight caused such a strong emotion in the viewer "that a picture of her was impressed in the electromagnetic field of the streamlet." Lethbridge had caught sight of the original impression.

Later Lethbridge learned that the mill owner had seen a ghost on the hill. It was a man, dressed in the fashion of forty years ago. It was obvious to Lethbridge that his ghost and the mill owner's ghost had, when alive, been happy to see each other. Each had impressed a picture of the other on the one field of force.

it was pointing toward the sky. (For some people a dowsing rod reacts by pointing upward, for others it dips downward.)

I wondered if the strain on my fingers was causing the rod to point upward. I tried the experiment of making it dip down instead. It refused. I tried holding it so tight that it could not move. It was impossible. As I passed over the same spot, it twisted up so strongly that I could not hold it still.

The power was particularly strong in the centre of the circle. I asked my friend what this meant, and he said he did not know. It could mean water, but this was unlikely because we kept getting the same reaction all around the stone circle at a point just beyond the outer perimeter.

I do not know what this force is. All I can say, with complete confidence, is that it exists.

Lethbridge believed that these "earth forces" can be increased and intensified by generations of worship and religious sacrifice. This could explain why his hand began to tingle when he placed it on the stone.

The Merry Maidens is discussed by John Michell in his book *The Old Stones of Lands End*. Michell points out that this whole area is covered with *leys* – the "old straight tracks" or lines first observed by Alfred Watkins. The Merry Maidens is the focus of such a system of leys. You can draw neat straight lines from its centre through other local landmarks, like ancient *barrows* (prehistoric burial mounds) and other standing stones. Michell has suggested that leys are identical with the ancient Chinese dragon paths. If this is so, it seems just conceivable that when the dowsing rods twisted in my hands, I was experiencing the magnetic force of the dragon paths, and that the power which made the rods twist so violently at the centre of the circle springs from the union of several dragon paths at this point.

One of the first people to notice the alignment of ancient sites in the area of the Merry Maidens was the eminent British astronomer Sir Norman J. Lockyer, who wrote a book on Stonehenge and other British stone circles in the early years of this century. Lockyer's theory was that such monuments were not merely religious centres, but also sophisticated astronomical observatories. When certain stars came into alignment with a particular stone and the top of a burial mound, Lockyer suggested, the ancient priests would know that it was time for a certain religious ceremony or sacrifice.

When Lockyer first published his theory, it aroused scepticism and even downright hostility among scientists. Many objected that ancient cultures lacked the knowledge to construct anything so complicated. In recent years, however, Lockyer's theory has been revived by scientists like Alexander Thom, Professor of Engineering Science at Oxford University, and Gerald Hawkins, Professor of Astronomy at Boston University. As a result of their research, an increasing number of scientists now accept that Stonehenge, the Merry Maidens, and other megalithic monuments like Carnac in northwest France, were designed as astronomical observatories. Even more amazing was the discovery that astronomical measurements made in these observatories were of incredible accuracy. For example, the moon deviates from its regular course by an almost imperceptible amount – 0.9° over a long period. Yet when Hawkins and Thom studied the methods of observation used by the builders of Stonehenge and Callanish (a stone circle in the Outer Hebrides), they discovered that this minute deviation of 0.9° had been recognized more than 3000 year ago. It was not discovered by modern astronomers until the sixteenth century.

Why should prehistoric man want to observe the heavens so minutely? Why should he want to construct an observatory that is also a church? There can be no doubt that sites such as Stonehenge were used for religious observances. Of course, many modern churches are constructed so that the window behind the altar catches the light of the rising sun; but that is purely for dramatic effect. It would certainly cause comment if we installed computers behind the altars of our cathedrals, or used the towers to house astronomical telescopes.

The explanation almost certainly lies in the ancient science of astrology. It seems likely that the builders of Stonehenge and other such temples believed that there were certain times of the year when the stars were propitious for the performance of religious rites, and when the hidden forces of the earth could be harnessed for religious purposes. Our ancestors observed that the tides are affected by the moon, and that certain people become "lunatics" at the time of the full moon. They believed that the hidden forces of the earth also rise and fall according to the movements of the heavenly bodies. For example, an eclipse of the moon affects the level of the earth's magnetism; and this may have been why prehistoric astronomers attached particular importance to the prediction of eclipses. The very sacredness of a sacred place like Stonehenge would reach a maximum intensity at periods when the influence of the heavenly bodies on the earth's forces were strongest. These would be the obvious times for major religious rites.

The moon, being closer to the earth, has a greater influence on phenomena such as tides. Therefore we might expect our ancestors to be more concerned with the observation of the moon than of the stars. This, according to Professor Hawkins, is precisely the case.

Tom Lethbridge became convinced that there are at least three distinct varieties of magnetic field – one associated with water, one with mountains and one with deserts and other open spaces. The theory of water fields – or "naiad fields", as Lethbridge preferred to call them – came about as a result of the experience on Ladram Beach which has already been described. The "ghoul", he believed, was a kind of tape recording of the suicide's misery.

Lethbridge's theory could be the key to a mysterious death that occurred in England in 1939. On the morning of 10 May searchers found the body of Harry Dean lying at the foot of a boulder in an abandoned quarry on the slopes of Bredon Hill, Gloucestershire. On the previous evening, Dean had gone for a stroll on Bredon Hill. When he failed to return home his wife notified the police.

The strange thing was that there was no obvious cause for death. Since Dean was lying on the floor of the quarry, the likeliest explanation was that he had fallen from the surrounding cliff some fifty feet above; but the body was unbruised. A post mortem examination revealed the astonishing fact that he had been strangled by his own tie. The coroner concluded that Dean had climbed the three-foot-high boulder at whose foot he was found, and that he had slipped and displaced the cartilage of his leg. He had fainted and been choked by his tie.

There was never any suggestion that Dean had been the victim of foul play. Nothing was missing from his pockets, and there were no signs of a struggle. Yet it seemed extraordinary that an accidental fall from a boulder only three feet high could result in a man's death.

The sheer improbability of the coroner's explanation led local author Harold Wilkins to undertake his own investigation. He deliberately waited a whole year until May 1940 so that conditions would be as similar as possible to those at the time of Harry Dean's death. He then visited the quarry with his brother. The first thing Wilkins noticed about Death Quarry was that its floor had evidently been levelled many centuries before the site's use as a quarry, which archaeologists have dated at around 750 BC. On this flat floor at the four points of the compass, Wilkins noticed four weathered boulders. Dean's body had been found by the one at the south end.

Wilkins and his brother made their way out of the quarry, up a grass-embanked causeway with unopened Stone Age barrows, past two ancient obelisks known as the "King and Queen stones", to the Iron Age fort on the top of Bredon Hill. This fort dates from the fifth century BC, and excavations have uncovered the skeletons of fifty men who had died in battle and had been mutilated by the enemy. Their heads, arms, and legs had been chopped off. In one corner of the fort stands a strange cracked stone known as the Bambury Stone. Archaeological evidence suggests that this was once an object of religious worship, perhaps an altar for sacrificial victims. Wilkins clambered onto the Bambury Stone to be photographed by his brother. As he did so, both men heard a sudden thud, as if a heavy object had fallen on the grass above them. Intrigued and puzzled, they searched the ground. It was a still, clear day, but they were unable to find anything that could account for the noise. "Something eerie and sinister had demonstrated its presence and its objection to the photographing of this weird stone," says Wilkins. He goes on to suggest that Harry Dean was strangled by some "unseen entity" as he stood at the foot of the boulder. Wilkins points out that Bredon Hill forms a rough quadrilateral with other hills. In another corner stands Long Compton Hill with its circle of megaliths known as the Rollright Stones, used as the site of witches' sabbaths in the Middle Ages. In a third corner of the quadrilateral is Meon Hill, again associated with black magic and witchcraft, and also with the apparition of a black dog. Wilkins suggests that such sites are imbued with dark and violent forces associated with pagan religious rites. Significantly, the priests of ancient Britain held one of their most important rituals in early May – just when Harry Dean met his death.

It is impossible to say whether Harry Dean's death was simply an unusual accident. It is doubtful that Lethbridge would have accepted the theory that Dean's death was due to some unseen entity. But he might well have agreed that it was caused by a sudden and violent fear – a ghoul.

The chief problem concerning the enigmas discussed so far in this book is that they seem to have so little in common. What possible connection could there be between the disappearance of a British regiment into a cloud, the strange loss of electric power in the Bermuda Triangle, and a feeling of "something nasty" on a Dorset beach? Many of the writers on the Bermuda Triangle talk about "space-time paradoxes", and suggest that the disappearing planes and ships might have tumbled into another dimension. Link this with dowsing experiences and we may be getting somewhere. The whole idea of strange forces connected with fields – whether these are ancient Chinese dragon paths or Lethbridge's ghouls – might offer some *practical* possibility of investigation. There is nothing to prevent readers of this book from making themselves dowsing rods or pendulums, and checking whether these ideas have any basis in fact.

Lethbridge himself embarked upon such a careful course of experiment, and his results are startling and fascinating. I myself have performed some of the simpler experiments, and can confirm that they actually work.

In a book by Lethbridge called *The Monkey's Tail*, readers can find a whole table of "rates" for various objects and qualities – milk, youth, apple, iron, alcohol, and so on. But they may be puzzled to see that the table includes such concepts as north, east, south, and west, life, death, danger, and time. How on earth do you hold the pendulum above "time"? Lethbridge explains that all you have to do is to think about a concept clearly, and then lengthen the string of the pendulum, which can be wound on a bobbin, until it gyrates. For example, if you think of the concept of anger, the pendulum will gyrate at forty inches precisely, because forty inches is the rate for anger. This idea may be less absurd than it sounds. Whenever you "see" anything, you do so by *firing* your attention toward it, as you might fire an arrow at a target. For example, if you look at your watch while thinking of something else, you simply do not register the time. We have all had the experience of staring straight at an object we have been looking for, and not seeing it. In order to see it, we need to reach out toward it with an "intention." Lethbridge is merely saying that this intention is the essential element in the use of the pendulum. The force that makes the pendulum circle or the dowsing rod twist in your hand may exist "out there", but it connects up with something in your mind.

Lethbridge discovered that the rate for "life" is twenty

inches. The rate for death, which is twice that, appeared to be a limit, since all substances tested had rates between one and forty. There was, however, a curious paradox. Lethbridge found that if he went beyond the limit of forty inches, the pendulum reacted again when it hit a figure that was the sum of something's own rate plus forty. For example, when testing a male the pendulum reacted at twenty-four inches, but it also reacted at sixty-four inches – forty plus twenty-four. Similarly all the other substances reacted at their own rate, and at their own rate plus forty.

In making this discovery Lethbridge encountered an even stranger phenomenon. If you take an object such as a walnut salad bowl, place it on the floor, and hold the pendulum over it, you will get a reaction at the specified rate for walnut: ten and a half inches. If you lengthen the pendulum to fifty and a half inches, you again get a reaction, *but not in the same place*. It is as if there were another salad bowl at the side of the real physical object. Lethbridge declares that this is always so – as if the object had a second position in another plane.

Equally curious is the test for "time." The pendulum fails to give a reaction for time below forty inches. But if you lengthen the string, you locate time at sixty inches (forty plus twenty, or the rate for death plus the rate for life). Lethbridge makes the strange observation that the time thus located "appears to be static." (The pendulum gives different reactions for things that are static and things that are changing or in motion.) His conclusion is that time does not register in our physical dimension because it is always passing. But *beyond* our dimension – beyond the point of death – we encounter another kind of time that is somehow static. Lethbridge admits that he cannot begin to grasp this possibility, and that he may have reasoned incorrectly from the information supplied by the pendulum. But in that case, he has no doubt that the fault lies in him, not in the pendulum.

Admittedly, this reasoning sounds wildly absurd, and the sceptical reader will remain totally unconvinced. After all, it is only too easy to make a pendulum change its swing from an arc to a circle by tiny unconscious movements of the fingers. Yet most people will accept the reality of dowsing, which has been seen to produce results. According to Lethbridge, the use of a pendulum enables the mind to establish contact with the "other dimension". Yet most dowsers agree that dowsing consists of tuning in to a "field." Is it possible that there are spots on the earth's surface where such fields are created by freak conditions, manifesting themselves as a kind of whirlpool in our space-time continuum? If so, we might expect objects that pass too close to be sucked into the whirlpool and to reappear later, floating on the surface of our normal time-sea. And if this idea creates a slight sense of vertigo, that is perhaps what you might expect of a whirlpool in space-time.

• chapter six •

UNINVITED VISITORS

L ough Nahooin is a small brown-coloured lake in Connemara on
the west coast of Ireland. At seven o'clock on the evening of 22
February 1968 Stephen Coyne, a local farmer, was walking along the
shores of the lough. He was accompanied by his eight-year-old son and
his dog. Stopping beside a heap of peat, Coyne saw a black object in the
water, and assumed that his dog had gone for a swim. When he
whistled, however, the dog came running from the opposite direction
and, on seeing the black object began to bark furiously. The farmer
looked more closely and saw that the object was some kind of animal
with a long neck and shiny black skin. When it plunged its head under
the surface, two humps appeared. The farmer also caught a glimpse of
a flat tail. By this time the barking of the dog had attracted the
attention of the "monster"; it began to swim towards the shore, its
mouth open. Alarmed for the safety of his dog, the farmer hurried
toward the water. At this the creature turned and made off. The eight-
year-old boy ran back to the nearby farm, and brought his mother and
the four other Coyne children. The family stood at the edge of the
lough watching the monster until it became too dark to see. Describing it later to an investigator, F.W. Holiday, the Coynes said the
monster was about twelve feet long. It had no eyes, but there were two
horns like those of a snail on top of its head.

Holiday was the author of a book on the famous Loch Ness
monster, which he believed to be some kind of giant slug. From
the descriptions of the Coyne family, he had no doubt that this

Lough Nahooin monster was another member of the same species. Since Lough Nahooin is a mere 100 yards long – compared with the twenty-four miles of Loch Ness – there seemed a reasonable chance of catching the Irish lake monster. Accordingly, Holiday's team brought nets, support-buoys, and 100 yards of heavy chain to Lough Nahooin. They stretched the nets across the middle of the lake, and then rowed around the lake firing a heavy rifle into the water to force the monster to rush into the nets. Nothing happened – except that Holiday developed a severe toothache. After several disappointing days, they abandoned the hunt. Nevertheless, Holiday remained convinced that the monster had been in the lake all the time – and is there still.

Holiday himself has acknowledged the obvious argument against his idea. Lough Nahooin is full of trout, and if a creature even the size of a crocodile lived there, the fish would all be eaten in a matter of weeks. Perhaps, then, the Coyne family mistook an otter or a large eel for the monster. Even if that were so in this case, there have been numerous sightings of some unknown species in many of the peaty lakes in the west of Ireland. Holiday gathered further evidence from Georgina Carberry, the librarian of Clifden in Connemara. In 1954 Miss Carberry and three friends drove to nearby Lough Fadda, a mile-and-a-half-long lake, to fish for trout. They settled down on a tongue of land to have a picnic. Then they saw the monster, which at first they took to be a man swimming. The creature moved toward them in a leisurely manner, and they could see two large humps and a forked tail. They also saw a huge sharklike mouth, although none of them noticed teeth. When they became alarmed and moved away from the edge of the lake, the creature turned and swam away. Georgina Carberry found the experience so unpleasant that she kept looking back as they drove away to see if the monster was following them. She suffered from nightmares for weeks afterwards, and one of her companions subsequently had a mental breakdown. Miss Carberry described the creature's movements as "wormy". Other witnesses who have reported seeing monsters in nearby lakes generally agree on an undulating worm-like movement.

Our original objection remains to all such monster sightings: how could creatures of the size described exist in these tiny lakes? Many writers on the Loch Ness monster have made the same point. It is true that Loch Ness is twenty-four miles long, but it is only a mile wide. There would have to be more than one monster for the species to survive, and a colony of monsters would soon eat all the fish and die of starvation.

A few months after his visit to Lough Nahooin, Holiday was browsing through a book on Babylonian history by Sir Wallis Budge. He came across a Babylonian creation myth that described how the god Anu had created marshes. According to the ancient text, "the marshes created the Worm. And the Worm said: '. . . Let me drink amongst the teeth, and set me on the gums, that I may devour the blood of the teeth . . .'" Holiday recalled the strange and persistent toothache that had begun as soon as he arrived at Lough Nahooin, and which vanished as soon as he left the area. He experienced a sudden absurd suspicion: could it be that the monster was not a creature of flesh and blood, *but some kind of a ghost*?

Of course, the idea sounds preposterous. But before we dismiss it, let us recall a point made by T.C. Lethbridge: a ghost is not necessarily a supernatural spirit. The image you see on your television screen is a kind of ghost. It is a mere "spectre" of something that may be happening in a studio many miles away. Lethbridge firmly believed that the ghost of the woman he saw near his home was some kind of tape recording. Carl G. Jung, one of the most eminent psychologists of our time, made a similar suggestion about flying saucers. He thought that the saucers could be *projections* of some deep unconscious need in mankind. Jung does not mean that UFOs are mere illusions, based on some form of wishful thinking; he means that some deep religious craving in the subconscious mind of the whole race may somehow project the image of UFOs so that they actually appear in the outside world.

Holiday reached the conclusion that UFOs and monsters share the characteristic of being less solid and real than they look. At least he can claim to have had experience of both. In his book *The Dragon and the Disk* he describes a number of sightings of UFOs and of the Loch Ness monster. The first UFO he saw, when fishing on the Welsh coast, resembled a cloud "of shiny blue-grey cotton wool", orbiting slowly in a circle. A week later, driving along a mountain road in Wales, he saw another such "cloud" and examined it through binoculars. The cloud was oval and about twenty-five feet long. Similar clouds have been described by witnesses over Loch Ness.

Holiday was fascinated by how often the two themes of "dragons" and "disks" appear in ancient cultures. He points

Loch Ness Monster

out that many Bronze Age barrows, when seen from the air, resemble flying saucers. Drawings of disklike objects are found all over the world in caves of the Palaeolithic period between 12,000 and 30,000 years ago. Equally common are drawing of worms or dragons. These also turn up frequently in carvings in old churches, and usually appear to symbolize the power of evil. Holiday's suggestion is that some of our remote ancestors worshipped disks, while others worshipped dragons or serpents. The disks usually seem to be associated with good, and the dragons are almost invariably evil.

Anyone who has ever taken an interest in UFOs knows that they have a curious habit of appearing and disappearing. Ivan Sanderson, who also wrote on the Bermuda Triangle, described a UFO he and his wife saw in 1958. It was an oval object that "was sort of flashing on and off, from almost total diaphaneity to complete solidity, at about three flashes per second." That is to say, it appeared solid one moment, and almost invisible the next. There have been dozens of reports of flying saucers that have "vanished into thin air" – giving rise to the theory that they have slipped out of our space-time into another dimension. Creatures like the Loch Ness monster seem to have the same irritating characteristic. For the past few years a Loch Ness investigation team has kept constant watch at the loch throughout the summer, with their cameras loaded. During that time the monster has been seen repeatedly – by members of the team and others – yet hardly ever photographed with any degree of success. Frustrated monster-watchers have sometimes wondered if the creature has a malicious sense of humor.

Many psychical investigators have entertained the same suspicion about ghosts and poltergeists. Holiday describes a case that he investigated in Wales. Some friends had leased a house that appeared to be haunted. Electric lights turned themselves on and off, footsteps walked down empty corridors, voices were heard, and a shadowy figure was seen in the house and the garden. The Society for Psychical Research was consulted. They suggested that the various phenomena might be due to the vibration of the tides *five miles away*. Careful experiment convinced Holiday that no amount of vibration could make a light turn itself on – as it did when he sat drinking tea with his friends. Nor could vibrations cause doorknobs to turn as they often did when no one was standing anywhere near them.

Anybody who has experienced such strange events at first

hand is bound to ask himself the question: where do ghosts or poltergeists come from? Are they projections of our subconscious mind or of someone else's subconscious mind? Are they actually here, in our world, but invisible except in special circumstances? Do they exist in some way outside our normal dimensions of space and time? If so, do they originate in that same world that many ufologists believe to be the home of flying saucers? In the present state of our knowledge, we cannot answer these questions; but we can go on asking them and trying to find the answers.

Holiday admits that his own case is far from complete. Some essential pieces of the jigsaw are missing. What he is suggesting – purely as a working hypothesis – is that there could be some connection between UFOs, lake monsters, and certain psychical phenomena. The dragon and disk symbolism that occurs in so many pre-Christian religions seems to indicate that the ancient priesthoods recognized the connection. We do not yet possess the knowledge to penetrate their secrets. But we do have an ever increasing mass of data about modern dragons and disks, some of which suggests a definite link between UFOs and psychical phenomena. Holiday cites the case of Annabelle Randall who, on the night of 7 October 1965, was driving her fiancé John Plowman back to his home near Warminster about fifteen miles from Stonehenge. Toward midnight they approached a railroad bridge near Heytesbury, Wiltshire, where there had been a number of fatal road accidents. In the beam of their headlights they saw a body sprawled at the roadside with its legs in the road. When they stopped the car and went to investigate, the body vanished. An hour later on her return journey, Miss Randall again passed under the bridge. As she did so, she saw a large orange ball that shot into the sky. At the same time, she saw two figures walking along the road toward her. They wore dark clothes and some sort of headgear, and the lower half of their bodies glistened as if wet.

A month later, a retired Royal Air Force Group Captain and his wife had a similar experience when driving about a mile from the bridge at one thirty in the morning. They saw a tall figure wearing a mask. Then a man staggered out of the hedge. He was covered in blood, and seemed to be an accident victim. By the time they had stopped the car and reversed, both men had vanished. The Group Captain told his story to the Features Editor of the *Warminster Journal* and to a BBC producer, but asked for his name to be withheld.

Holiday makes an interesting suggestion concerning such
"phantom accidents". He observes that more UFOs have been
seen in the area around Stonehenge than anywhere else in
Britain. He adds that the first UFO he sighted over the Welsh
coast moved away due east, towards the little mining village of
Aberfan. It was there on 21 October 1966 – just thirteen days
after his sighting – that a massive coal tip slid downhill, killing
128 children and sixteen adults. Holiday points out that in
Celtic and Norse mythology, the souls of those who died in
battle are conducted to the Underworld by special messengers
of the dead, called *Valkyries* by the Norse. These messengers are
usually represented as wearing unusual headgear – a kind of
pointed helmet. Is it conceivable, Holiday asks, that the strange
figures seen on the Warminster road were also "messengers of
the dead", whose business is to perform some kind of psychic
first aid on those who have died in violent accidents? And
might the old legends of Valkyries and similar creatures have
been based on the visitation of UFOs and their strange inhabitants?

Curiously enough, T.C. Lethbridge arrived independently at
a similar theory shortly before his death in 1973. He published
it in his last book, *The Legend of the Sons of God*. Lethbridge is
careful to state that his conclusions are purely speculative, but
they have a bearing on Holiday's Valkyries and it is worth
examining what Lethbridge has to say on the subject.

Lethbridge's starting point is the mystery of ancient stone
monuments like Stonehenge and the Merry Maidens. When he
tested a stone at the Merry Maidens with his pendulum, the
reaction was violent. Other prehistoric monuments produced a
similar reaction. Lethbridge became convinced that the power
that apparently emanates from such monoliths is a form of
energy that comes from living creatures. He calls it *bio-energy*,
or bio-electricity. He believes that such energy can be generated
by the frenzied kind of dancing that forms part of many ancient
religious rituals. This bio-energy, he maintains, can be stored in
stone monoliths and in trees – and it was a vital link with
visitors from other worlds.

In recent years, writers like Erich von Däniken have popu-
larized the theory that the earth was visited by flying saucers in
the remote past, and that accounts of these visits can be found
in many ancient texts including the Bible. Lethbridge had
already completed his *Legend of the Sons of God* when a friend
sent him von Däniken's first book *Chariots of the Gods?*, contain-

ing this now-famous theory. Lethbridge's first reaction was to decide not to publish his own book. Then it struck him that many of his own conclusions differed so fundamentally from von Däniken's that it would have been a pity to consign them to the wastepaper basket.

Lethbridge had concluded that monuments like Stonehenge were intended to be signal beacons for some form of spacecraft. He suggests that the inhabitants of the UFOs understood the uses to which bio-energy could be put. They therefore encouraged the men of the Bronze Age to build these giant monuments, and to keep them highly charged with bio-energy to enable the UFOs to home in on them.

While we must admit that Lethbridge's theory sounds wildly speculative, we have to acknowledge that such monuments as Stonehenge present us with a baffling mystery. When modern engineers set about replacing one of the giant lintels at Stonehenge, they had the full benefit of modern cranes and lifting equipment, and the operation was still a difficult and costly one. Yet we know that our primitive ancestors not only succeeded in erecting these gigantic stones, but that they had transported them enormous distances across wild and rugged country. Either the ancient builders possessed a far higher degree of engineering knowledge than the traditional view of their culture suggests – or they were instructed and directed by beings from a more advanced civilization. The immense avenues of standing stones in Carnac, Brittany, present a similar problem. It is worth noting that their layout strongly supports the idea that they were aerial markers.

If the Earth had been visited by aliens in the distant past, where did these beings come from? There is a certain amount of evidence in ancient mythology – for example, in the legends of Easter Island – that suggests that the answer might be Mars or Venus or both. The astronomer Professor Carl Sagan believes that Mars could have been inhabited as recently as 1000 years ago. However, Lethbridge has another suggestion to make, based on the evidence of the pendulum. His suggestion indicates that there are other levels of existence beyond this one. If there are other levels, says Lethbridge, is it not conceivable that there are people living on them?

In addition to the evidence of the pendulum, Lethbridge produces many arguments in favor of these other levels based on out-of-the-body experiences and the power of certain mediums to foretell the future. He puts forward another fascinating idea. The pendulum appears to show that the other levels possess a higher rate of vibration than our earthly level, as if their energies were of a higher frequency. Yet the pendulum apparently enables us to establish some sort of contact with these levels. Perhaps, Lethbridge suggests, it might be possible for scientists to construct a machine that would alter our vibrational rate, and so make these levels directly accessible. Such a machine, he says, "would necessitate some kind of dynamo to produce a field of force around the experimenters. . ." Lethbridge would therefore seem to agree with F.W. Holiday and many ufologists that Unidentified Flying Objects could originate on some other plane of existence. Lethbridge also points out that if these other levels are characterized by a higher vibrational rate of energy, then creatures from these levels could actually be walking among us now – completely invisible to us. They would become visible only if their vibrational rate were suddenly slowed down. This can be grasped by means of a simple analogy. If a train on which you are riding goes through a station too fast, you cannot read the name of the station. If the train were travelling extremely fast, you would not even notice the station. On the other hand, to beings on other planes, we would appear to be travelling much more slowly than they – as if we were living in slow motion – and we would therefore be clearly visible to them. *They* could visit us by slowing down their vibrational rate, but we cannot at present visit them – except possibly by dying.

It is interesting to note that, if Lethbridge is right, our thought vibrations would have difficulty in grasping the nature of reality because they are too slow. But the faculty we call intuition seems to operate instantaneously, on a higher wavelength. This may explain why intuition has the power to grasp complex realities beyond the range of our everyday thought.

Lethbridge's machine for travelling to other planes sounds like pure science fiction. Yet there are many students of ufology who are convinced that such a machine has actually been built and tested. Unfortunately, one of the most important witnesses, the astronomer and mathematician Morris K. Jessup, is dead. Jessup taught at the University of Michigan, and was sent by the Carnegie Institute to study the Inca remains in Peru and the Aztec ruins in Mexico. The study of these ancient constructions led him to the conclusion that they might well have been erected with the aid of outer space visitors, whose aim was partly to create landing markers for spacecraft. He published his theory in 1955 in *The Case for the UFO*, one of the first great classics on the subject of flying saucers. In this book, Jessup also suggested that many of the strange disappearances of ships and planes in the Bermuda Triangle – and mysteries such as those of the *Mary Celeste* and *Ellen Austin* – could have been due to some kind of UFO activity.

After the publication of his book, Jessup was contacted by someone who claimed to be a survivor of an incredible experiment conducted by the U.S. Navy in 1943. Known as "the Philadelphia Experiment", it was supposed to have resulted in the death of some participants and the mental breakdown of others. When Jessup began to investigate the affair, the Navy asked him if he would be interested in working on a similar project. Jessup declined. In 1959 Jessup was found dead in his car, asphyxiated by exhaust gas. There are some who believe that his suicide was staged, and that he was killed before he could publicize ideas arising out of the experiment.

In *The Mysterious Unknown*, Robert Charroux cites another version of the Philadelphia Experiment, as reported from the Soviet Union. The Soviets apparently believed that the U.S. Navy was investigating some magnetic version of the Moebius strip. This strip is a "one-sided" ring of paper, and is easy to make. You simply take a long strip of paper, give one of its ends a half-twist, and then glue the two ends of the strip together to form a ring. If you wish to verify that this strip has only one side, take a pencil, and draw a line down the center of the strip. You will find that, without having to turn the ring inside out, you can continue the line until it has rejoined its beginning. If you take a pair of scissors and cut along the penciled line, the strip will unfold into one large ring instead of the two inter-linked rings that most people expect.

According to the Soviet version, the vessel used in the Philadelphia Experiment was a submarine, and the Moebius strip consisted of a powerful magnetic field. As the submarine pursued its course around this invisible strip – turning over completely in the course of each revolution – an electronic device was used to cut the field in two, as if with a pair of scissors. At this point the submarine vanished, to reappear miles away. In the Soviet version, as in the American one, some of the crew died and others became insane. The story was told by Professor Doru Todericiu, who claimed to have read it in official reports published in the Soviet Union.

Whatever the real story behind the Philadelphia Experiment,

it is interesting that both the Soviet and American versions are based on the use of a magnetic field of unusual power. There is also a postscript to Jessup's account of the experiment, as related by Dr Manson Valentine, that has the touch of authenticity. Jessup was apparently told that, on two occasions, the ship's binnacle (compass box) burst into flames as it was being carried ashore, with disastrous results to the carrier.

We know that magnetism affects compasses – but why should it cause a wooden box to burst into flame? The answer may well lie in Lethbridge's ideas about bio-electricity. Lethbridge had said from the first that bio-electricity can be generated by dancing. Perhaps this is related to spontaneous combustion. For example a girl, dancing in a London nightclub with her boyfriend, suddenly erupted into flames, and died on her way to the hospital. There were no flames in the room. Her dancing partner declared that the flames seemed to burst from the girl's back, chest, and shoulders, setting her hair on fire. Hundreds of similar cases have been recorded. Like all other energies known to man, bio-electricity seems to have its dangerous side. But it may also provide science with another angle in the investigation of the strange unknown powers of the human psyche.

chapter seven

CURSES AND JINXES

The year was 1928. The city, Kobe, Japan. A middle-aged English couple, the C.J. Lamberts, stood in front of a junk shop window. "That's what I'd like," said Marie Lambert, pointing to a tiny statuette of a half-naked fat man seated on a cushion. She recognized the laughing man as Ho-tei, the Japanese god of Good Luck. "Let's find out what he costs," said her husband, as they walked into the shop. They were pleasantly surprised to find that the statuette was cheap, even though it was made of ivory. It seemed almost too good to be true. Back on their cruise ship, the Lamberts examined their purchase closely. The statuette had the creamy colour of old ivory, and was beautifully carved. As far as they could see, its only imperfection was a small hole underneath. The carver had apparently used the base of an elephant's tusk for the statue, and there was a tiny hole where the nerve of the animal's tooth had ended. This had been plugged neatly with an ivory peg. Altogether, the statuette seemed to be one of those rare bargains that tourists dream about.

Marie Lambert stowed the statuette in her luggage, and the ship sailed to Manila. On the second day out, Mrs Lambert began to suffer from a toothache. The ship's doctor prescribed painkillers, but they did little good. The next twelve days were miserable for both the Lamberts. In Manila, before Mrs Lambert could visit a dentist, she and her husband contracted an unpleasant fever whose chief symptom was pain in all the joints. When Marie Lambert finally got to a dentist, his drill slipped and drove through to the nerve of her tooth, increasing her pain instead of curing it.

On the next lap of the voyage, which took the ship to Australia, the god of luck figurine was somehow transferred to Mr Lambert's luggage. The following day, he was prostrated with an agonizing toothache. In Cairns, Australia, he went to a dentist, who told him there was nothing wrong with his teeth. In fact, the ache had stopped while he was at the dentist's. But it started again as soon as he got back to his cabin. Two days later, he consulted another dentist, and the same thing happened. In Brisbane, he ordered a dentist to start pulling out his teeth, and to keep on pulling until the pain stopped. When the first tooth came out, the pain went away. It started again as soon as Lambert returned to the ship.

In Sydney the Lamberts left their luggage in bond. The toothache ceased. On the voyage to New Zealand, the luggage was in their cabin only once, when they repacked; Lambert's toothache started again. Then the luggage went to the hold, and the pain stopped. In New Zealand, while on shore, he had no toothache. There was only one short bout of toothache on the continuing trip to Chile – when the Lamberts repacked their luggage in the cabin. In the United States, the couple visited Lambert's mother. She was so delighted with Ho-tei that they made her a present of the little god. When her excellent teeth started aching a few hours later, she handed back the gift saying that she felt it was "bad medicine." The Lamberts still did not connect Ho-tei with their toothaches.

Their first suspicion occurred on the way across the Atlantic to Britain. A fellow passenger who was interested in ivory borrowed Ho-tei overnight to show her husband. In the morning, she told the Lamberts that she and her husband had both had toothaches. The Lamberts thought about their own toothaches, and realized that they had always occurred when Ho-tei was in their cabin. Marie Lambert wanted to throw the statuette overboard. Her husband was afraid that the god might retaliate by rotting every tooth in their heads. So they took Ho-tei back to London with them. Lambert took the figure to an oriental art shop and showed it to the Japanese manager, who immediately offered to buy it. Lambert explained that he could not take money for the statuette, and he described the troubles it seemed to have caused. The manager sent for an old man in Japanese national costume, and the two men examined the figure carefully. From what they told him, Lambert gathered that Ho-tei was a temple god. In the East, the statues of such gods are sometimes given "souls" – small medallions hidden inside them. This probably explained the ivory plug in the base of the figure. The old Japanese man placed Ho-tei in a shrine at the end of the shop and lit joss sticks in front of it. Then, with an expression of awe, he bowed Lambert out of the shop.

In the end, C.J. Lambert derived some small profit from his uncomfortable adventure. He recounted it in a travel book that made good sales. But he never revisited the London art shop.

Lambert's understandable assumption was that the god of luck had been taking revenge on unbelievers who had removed

The home of Eugene Binkowski of Rotterdam, New York, had a hum that never stopped. The family wasn't sure when it had started, but became aware of it after a series of illnesses had afflicted each of them. Not only did they have frequent headaches, earaches, and toothaches, but they also suffered from stiffness of the joints. Finally they realized that the source of the problems was a constant faint humming oound throughout the house. They reported the trouble to the police, who could not come up with any explanation.

It was natural that General Electric in nearby Schenectady should become interested in the sound mystery, so the next investigators were technicians from that firm. Using the latest equipment that they had at their command, they tested the house thoroughly. At the end of it, they claimed they could hear no sound of a peculiar nature in the house.

In desperation Binkowski wrote to the then President John Kennedy. A few days later some Air Force sound experts turned up with equipment designed to detect high frequency sounds. They could not trace the hum. The only bit of information they offered was that tests showed the whole family had especially acute hearing. It was possible, they said, for the Binkowskis to be hearing a sound at some unusual pitch. Despite the verdicts of the General Electric and Air Force experts, hundreds of visitors to the Binkowski home reported they could hear the hum. Some of them also felt the house to be mysteriously stuffy.

The Binkowskis endured the hum for about nine months without relief. They finally had to move out of the house and into a garage to escape it.

him from his temple. Yet there could be another explanation for this strange affair.

Around the Iron Age fort in Sidbury Castle in southern England, T.C. Lethbridge picked up many rounded flint pebbles of the kind commonly found on beaches. It seemed unlikely that the sea had transported the stones to the fort, which stands on the top of a hill three miles inland. However, the stones were like those used as slingshot in Iron Age times. Lethbridge tested the stones with a pendulum whose string extended to twenty-four inches – the male length. There was a strong reaction. He tested them again at forty inches – the rate for anger, war, and death. Once more the reaction was strong.

Lethbridge possessed some similar sling stones from the Iron Age camp in Wandlebury, south of Cambridge. These also gave the reaction for maleness, but not for war or anger. Stones of the same type collected from the beach gave no reaction either for maleness or war.

Lethbridge's conclusion was that the Wandlebury stones had only been used for practice shots – which seems likely, since Wandlebury had been an army camp in the Iron Age. The Sidbury stones had been used in actual warfare. Both groups of stones retained the impression of maleness caused by the men who had handled them. As a further test, Lethbridge took some of the stones from the beach and threw them against a wall. They then responded to the male rate of twenty-four inches. Stones thrown by his wife only responded to the female rate – twenty-nine inches. Some kind of thought energy – or biological electricity – had apparently impressed itself on the stones like a seal. And it seemed to last indefinitely.

According to Lethbridge, the pendulum can also reveal the *date* at which the thought field was implanted in an object. This is done by counting the number of times the pendulum revolves over the object before returning to its normal oscillation. Lethbridge established a date of 320 BC for all the Sidbury stones, and 220 BC for those from Wandlebury.

Lethbridge used a pendulum to establish who had last handled the stones. But there are certain human beings who can achieve the same result simply by contact with an object. They are called *psychometrists*. Two of the best-known modern psychometrists, Peter Hurkos and Gerard Croiset, have achieved considerable publicity by aiding the police in the

investigation of crimes. By holding an object associated with
the crime, such as a murder weapon, they have been able to
describe the crime, and often the criminal.

In the 1840s the Frenchman Alexis Didier revealed similar
powers. A report in the British *Medical Times* of 8 July 1844 tells
how Didier was given a small leather case belonging to a
certain Colonel Llewellyn. Didier placed the case against his
stomach, and was then able to tell the owner that it contained a
piece of bone – the colonel's own bone. He went on to describe
in detail the incident in which the colonel had been wounded,
even specifying the number of wounds he had received. The
records of the Society for Psychical Research contain dozens of
similar cases. These suggest that psychometry is a fairly
common human faculty – as common perhaps as the ability
to dowse, although less developed in most human beings.

What would have happened if Alexis Didier had held the statue
of Ho-tei? He might have experienced some of the fear and
agony of a dying elephant – and perhaps the appalling pain of
having a tusk removed before death. For a man of Didier's
sensitivity, the horror might have been almost unbearable. In
less sensitive human beings, the tooth-fragment might have
induced a milder form of psychic disturbance that manifested
itself as severe toothache. If so, according to Lethbridge's
theory, the statue of Ho-tei would still be capable of causing
toothache in another thousand years.

It is worth recalling that F.W. Holiday complained of a severe
toothache during his expedition to Lough Nahooin in search of
monsters, and that he subsequently discovered a Babylonian
text describing a supernatural worm whose activities include
"devouring the blood of the teeth". Is it conceivable that certain
negative psychic forces manifest themselves in the form of
toothache?

If the idea sounds absurd, it is largely because we have
ceased to think in terms of negative psychic forces. The peoples
of primitive tribes say that a person who experiences continual
misfortune is "accursed". We would call him "accident prone".
Our classification implies that proneness to accidents arises
from a person's own carelessness or nervous tension. We have
all known people who seem to attract bad luck – the kind of
people who happen to be walking past when the window-
cleaner drops a bucket. These people appear to be suffering
from other people's carelessness, or from plain undeserved

misfortune. Yet we still have the feeling that there is some connection between this kind of ill-luck and the personality of the sufferer. There may be something about the attitude of such people – a certain expectation that the worst will happen. This raises the interesting question of whether the accident is somehow triggered by their subconscious attitude. Everything we learn about the power of the mind suggests that thought fields may be altogether more influential than we have hitherto recognized.

The psychic investigator and journalist Edward Russell has suggested that there may be a connection between negative thought fields and the "curses" that appear to surround certain objects like the statuette of Ho-tei. Like Lethbridge, he believes that thought fields can implant themselves in objects, rather as magnetism or static electricity does, and create the same kind of patterns that an electric field can produce on a magnetic recording tape. Lethbridge had advanced the theory that negative thought fields – or ghouls as he called them – can imprint themselves on the magnetic field of water, and there is some evidence that ghouls may also imprint themselves on objects. We have already seen that the *Mary Celeste* was dogged by bad luck from the moment of her launching, and few sailors doubt that there are such things as "jinxed ships". In his book on sea mysteries, *Invisible Horizons*, Vincent Gaddis writes, "There are happy, gay ships, and there are others so impregnated with evil that they must be destroyed by fire."

The particular evil ship that Gaddis had in mind was the German battleship *Scharnhorst*, launched in October 1936. When only half completed, the ship rolled onto its side, killing sixty workmen. Hitler and Goering arrived for the final launching only to discover that the ship had somehow launched itself the previous night, destroying several barges. In the *Scharnhorst*'s first major engagement – the attack on Danzig in 1939 – one of the guns exploded, killing nine men, and the air supply system broke down, suffocating twelve gunners. A year later during the bombardment of Oslo, the *Scharnhorst* was badly damaged and had to be towed away. In the dark, she collided with the ocean liner *Bremen*, which settled into the river mud and was bombed to pieces by the British. The *Scharnhorst* was repaired and set sail for the Arctic in 1943, but during the voyage she passed a British patrol vessel which her crew failed to notice. The vessel radioed a warning. Several British cruisers quickly located the *Scharnhorst* and bombarded her. The

Howard Carter and Lord Carnarvon outside the steps of the tomb
thought to be cursed, the tomb of Tutankhamun

Scharnhorst fled, and it seemed she would escape her pursuers. But one British commander decided to try a last long shot on the off-chance of scoring a hit. The gamble paid. The *Scharnhorst* began to blaze, providing a target for more shells. The ship sank to the bottom with most of her crew. Yet the curse apparently lingered on. Weeks later, two survivors from the *Scharnhorst* were found on a beach. They were dead – killed by an emergency oil heater that had exploded when they tried to light it for warmth.

Misfortune also pursued the Lockheed Constellation airliner AHEM-4, starting on the day in July 1945 when a mechanic walked into one of the plane's propellors and was killed. Precisely one year later, on 9 July 1946, Captain Arthur Lewis died at the controls while the plane was flying in mid-Atlantic. Exactly one year after that, on 9 July 1947, a newly installed engine burst into flame shortly after takeoff. The captain, Robert Norman, extinguished the flames with a mechanical fire-extinguisher, but then found that the plane lacked the power to climb above the roof of an apartment building. Norman switched on the takeoff power and managed to climb out of danger. But when he tried to ease the power off again, the controls remained jammed. He and his copilot finally wrestled the controls back by sheer force, and landed the plane success-fully.

July 1948 passed uneventfully. But on 10 July 1949 the airliner crashed near Chicago, killing everyone on board including Captain Robert Norman.

There are many records of houses, and even cars, that seem to bring disaster to their owners. A famous example is the car in which the Archduke Francis Ferdinand, heir to the thrones of Austria and Hungary, was assassinated in 1914 – a murder that precipitated the outbreak of World War I. The Archduke's wife died with him. Shortly after the start of war, General Potiorek of the Austrian army came into possession of the car. A few weeks later he suffered a catastrophic defeat at Valjevo, and was sent back to Vienna in disgrace. He could not stand this, and he died insane.

The next owner of the car was an Austrian captain who had been on Potiorek's staff. Only nine days after taking over the car, he struck and killed two peasants, and then swerved into a tree and broke his neck.

At the end of the war, the Governor of Yugoslavia became the owner of the car. After four road accidents in four months –

one of which caused him to lose an arm – he sold the car to a doctor. Six months later, the car was found upside down in a ditch. The doctor had been crushed to death inside it. The car was next sold to a wealthy jeweller who owned it for only a year before he committed suicide. After a brief spell in the hands of another doctor – who seems to have been all too anxious to get rid of it – the car was sold to a Swiss racing driver. He was killed in a race in the Italian Alps when the car threw him over a wall. The next owner was a Serbian farmer. He stalled the car one morning, and persuaded a passing carter to give him a tow. Forgetting to turn off the ignition, the farmer became the car's ninth victim when the motor started up, smashed the horse and cart, and overturned on a bend. A garage owner, Tibor Hirshfeld, was the car's final owner. One day, returning from a wedding with six friends, Hirshfeld tried to overtake another car at high speed. He and four of his companions were killed. The car then was taken to a Vienna museum where it has been ever since.

An example of a house that seems to bring bad luck to its tenants is the castle of Miramar near Trieste. It was built in the mid-nineteenth century by Emperor Franz Josef of Austria, but its first occupant was his brother the Archduke Maximilian. Maximilian died in front of a firing squad in Mexico, and his wife became insane. Empress Elizabeth was the next resident of Miramar, living there with her son Rudolph. In 1889 Rudolph and his mistress committed suicide, and in 1898 the Empress was assassinated by an Italian anarchist who believed in Italian liberation from Austria.

The next in line for the Austrian throne was Rudolph's cousin the Archduke Francis Ferdinand, who went to live in the beautiful castle. The Archduke and his wife were both assassinated in 1914 – the murder that contributed to bringing about World War I. At the end of the war the Duke of Aosta moved into Miramar. He died in a prison camp in British East Africa during World War II. After this war two British Major Generals became residents of the castle of Miramar. Both died of heart attacks.

It has not gone unnoticed that many jinxes appear to begin with a death or deaths: workers died building the *Scharnhorst*; a mechanic was killed by a propellor of the Lockheed Constellation airliner; the Archduke Franz Ferdinand and his wife were assassinated in their car. Many sailors are convinced that the spirits of the dead are involved in jinxes. To support their contention, they point to the two most notorious jinx ships of the nineteenth century: the British vessels *Hinemoa* and *Great Eastern*.

On her maiden voyage in 1892, the *Hinemoa* carried a ballast of rubble from a London graveyard. During the voyage four sailors died of typhoid. The ship's first captain went insane, the second ended in prison, the third died of alcoholism, the fourth died in mysterious circumstances in his cabin, and the fifth committed suicide – all, according to the crew, because of the bad luck brought by the bones of the four dead crew members.

The *Great Eastern*, built by the famous Victorian engineer Isambard Kingdom Brunel, was in her time the largest – and the unluckiest – ship in the world. Brunel collapsed with a heart attack on her deck, and died soon after. A riveter and his boy assistant vanished without trace during the ship's construction. The ship proved so heavy that she defied all attempts to launch her; it took three months and dozens of hydraulic jacks to move her from her berth. On her maiden voyage, a steam escape valve was left closed, resulting in an explosion that scalded five men to death. A full account of her subsequent misfortunes – explosions, collisions, and accidents at sea – would occupy many pages. Finally, a mere fifteen years after launching, she was brought back to Milford Haven in Wales, where she rusted and blocked the shipping lane. Breaking her up proved almost as difficult as building her. It was necessary to invent the wrecker's iron ball, suspended on a giant chain, to reduce her to scrap in 1889. Inside the double hull, the demolition experts discovered the skeletons of the riveter and his boy apprentice, who had vanished when the ship was being built. Few people doubted that they had discovered the cause of the ship's misfortunes.

The theory of thought fields provides a plausible alternative to the supernatural explanation. The sailors on board the *Hinemoa* knew that the ballast had been taken from a graveyard; the men who sailed the *Great Eastern* on her maiden voyage knew that a riveter and his assistant had vanished, and had possibly been sealed up in the hull. The crew of the airliner AHEM-4 knew that a mechanic had walked into the propeller and had been cut to pieces. The subsequent owners of Francis Ferdinand's car knew that the Archduke and his wife had met violent deaths in it. Therefore, assuming that in each vehicle the original tragic event itself created a negative thought field, or ghoul, does it not seem likely that their knowledge of the tragedy *predisposed* people to tune in to that field? In other words, the jinx may have been partly due to the negative thought field, and partly to the fear and nervous tension of the people involved.

Sceptics will object that fear and tension alone might have been to blame, and that the jinxes could have been entirely psychological in origin. This possibility cannot be completely ruled out. But it still leaves us with a residue of cases in which the victim knew nothing about the ghoul. C.J. and Marie Lambert had no reason to connect the statue of Ho-tei with their toothache, for example. Lethbridge put forward the theory of ghouls after he and his wife had independently experienced acute feelings of depression on an apparently peaceful beach. Lethbridge was even convinced that the field of a ghoul is sharply defined. He describes a ruined house where it was possible to step in and out of the affected area, as if there were a line drawn on the ground. The likeliest explanation would therefore seem to be that there is some sort of interaction between the negative thought field and the people who react to it.

chapter eight

ANCIENT FORCES

*A*t the Kofuku temple in Nara, Japan, a resentful priest named Kurodo decided to play an embarrassing trick on his fellow priests. At the side of a pond near the temple, Kurodo set up a placard that read: "On 3 March, a dragon shall ascend from this pond." The effect was just what he had expected. News of the placard spread far and wide, and people talked of nothing but dragons. On 3 March the pond was surrounded by thousands of people from all the neighbouring provinces. The day was sunny and peaceful. By noon nothing had happened, and the priests were beginning to feel worried. If no dragon appeared, they would lose face. Suddenly, a cloud drifted across the sky. A wind sprang up. The day became darker, and a storm broke. Rain fell in torrents and lightning flashed. Before Kurodo's startled eyes, a smoky shape like an enormous black dragon rose out of the pond and up into the clouds. This story may or may not be true. It was written by the great Japanese author Akutagawa, who probably based it on a tradition of the Kofuku temple.

If Akutagawa's tale sounds incredible, consider this story, which is certainly fact. In May 1727 François de Pâris, a young deacon of Paris, died of malnutrition and exhaustion. He was famous for his ascetic practices and for his charities to the poor, and his coffin was followed by hundreds of mourners. After it had been placed behind the altar of the church of St Medard, a line of mourners filed past. One small boy, accompanied by his father, limped awkwardly on a crippled leg. As he placed a bunch of flowers on the coffin, he suddenly fell to the ground, gasping and kicking. He was apparently suffering from a fit. A few minutes later, the fit passed off. The boy sat up, and was helped to his feet. A look of astonishment came over his face. Suddenly he began to dance and shout for joy. The crippled leg – twisted since birth – was straight. As the spectators stared in amazement, an old woman shouted: "I can use it!" She was waving her cured arm, which had been paralyzed for twenty-five years. Many fell on their knees around the coffin of the saintly deacon and prayed.

The miracles continued, and became more astounding. All kinds of sick people touched the coffin, went into convulsions, and were cured. After the body of the saintly priest had been buried behind the high altar, the miracles took place in the cemetery outside. They were so remarkable that it is tempting to dismiss contemporary accounts of them as pure exaggerations. Yet documentary evidence – some of it written by physicians – seems to show otherwise. A Mademoiselle Coirin had a cancer that had eaten away most of her breast, and the odour was so appalling that no one could go near her. After kneeling at the "saints'" tomb, not only was she cured, but the breast showed no sign of ever having had a cancer. This sounds absurd, but doctors examined it and testified that it was so.

Cripples walked; the blind were made to see; tumors vanished. Even odder manifestations began to occur. A young girl named Gabrielle Moler went into convulsions, after which she begged the spectators to beat her with sticks. She felt no pain and showed no bruises. She had seemingly acquired some of the curious powers possessed by Hindu fakirs. Strong men could pound her with hammers, and she remained unhurt. She would thrust her face into a blazing fire, and withdraw it unburned; she would leave her feet in the fire until the shoes and socks were burned away, and withdraw her feet unscathed. Another *convulsionaire*, the name given to those who experienced convulsions at the tomb, cured horrible sores and ulcers by sucking them. One man, who had been crippled, experienced the urge to spin on one leg at tremendous speed while reading from a holy book. He did this twice a day. Another convulsionaire could bounce six feet into the air, like a rubber ball, even when weighed down with heavy chains. Dozens of other visitors to the tomb rolled in convulsions or allowed spectators to beat them, without visible ill-effects.

Stonehenge, Wiltshire – the remains of a druid temple

A magistrate went to the churchyard convinced that the whole affair was a fraud. What he saw made him change his mind. He wrote books about it, and suffered imprisonment for his convictions.

The authorities were worried and embarrassed by the wild scenes at St Medard. François de Pâris, the young deacon who had started it all, had belonged to a religious sect known as the Jansenists. They denied free will and believed that people could only be saved by Divine Grace. The Jesuits, the most powerful religious order in Paris, detested the Jansenists. Through their influence, the churchyard of St Medard was closed down in 1732, five years after the miracles began. Convulsionaires were persecuted, and the miracles ceased. Jansenism was made illegal, and finally died out.

What happened at St Medard is similar to what happened at the Kofuku temple pond. A large number of people became deeply convinced that miracles were about to occur, and it seems likely that the united force of their subconscious minds *made* the miracles happen. The first people who followed François de Pâris's coffin already regarded him as a saint capable of producing miracles – and the initial cures strengthened their conviction. However, the story of the dragon in the pond suggests that there could be another explanation. In China and Japan, the dragon is a creature of deep religious significance – like the lamb in Christian countries. This recalls F. W. Holiday's observations about the dragon symbolism in ancient cultures and the association of dragonlike creatures with lakes.

It is also possible that the church of St Medard was built on a site where, like Stonehenge and other megaliths, dragon paths or ley lines meet. This would explain the concentration of magnetic powers there. Unfortunately, we know little of the religion that led our early ancestors to build great stone monuments in sacred places. But it seems clear that the stones themselves played some vitally important part in the worship. The gigantic granite blocks of Stonehenge, of Baalbek in the Lebanon, and of a hundred other ancient temples were not dragged into position merely to satisfy the whim of some all-powerful ruler. They were apparently intended to be giant accumulators of magic power. In some strange way, this force was used. It is even possible that it was used to raise the stones into position.

How was this power harnessed? The answer must surely

lie in some mysterious interaction between the forces of the earth and the powers of the subconscious mind. It may well be that a similar interaction occurred on a smaller scale in the cemetery of St Medard. Medical science cannot explain how Gabrielle Moler resisted the blows of strong men and the heat of a blazing fire. We know that hypnosis can render people insensitive to pain, but it could not prevent Gabrielle Moler from being burned when she thrust her face and feet into the flames. Hypnotism alone cannot explain how a man loaded with heavy chains could bounce six feet into the air. We know that yogis possess these kinds of powers, but they are acquired only after years of arduous training. All we can say is that whatever occurred at St Medard conferred extraordinary powers on the convulsionaires – or perhaps merely enabled them to make use of powers that all human beings possess.

Knowledge of the ancient religion of the forces of earth has been lost in the mists of time. Yet we have some fascinating clues to its nature. Anyone who wants seriously to follow them up should turn to an extraordinary and complex work called *The White Goddess*, written in the 1940s by the British poet Robert Graves. Graves describes how he was reading *The Mabinogion*, a collection of ancient Welsh legends, when he came across a curious and apparently meaningless poem called *The Song of.Taliesin*. Suddenly, in a flash of inspiration, he realized that some of the most baffling lines of the poem were a series of medieval riddles, and that these riddles contained clues to an ancient Celtic system of knowledge. As he pursued his research into this knowledge, he discovered that it was not confined to Wales. It could be found in the poetry and mythology of ancient Greece, Phoenicia, Scandinavia, India, and Africa. *And it was always closely linked with the moon.*

This was in itself a fascinating insight, and it tied in with a theory put forward twenty years earlier by the anthropologist Margaret Murray. In the early 1920s, Dr Murray had startled the academic world with a book called *The God of the Witches*. In it she had argued that what we now call witchcraft was actually an ancient pagan religion, whose chief deity was the moon goddess Diana. The ancient priests of Diana worshipped her by performing dances in which they wore animal skins and deer antlers on their heads. Christianity tried to stamp out this pagan religion, but it continued in secret. In Christian mythology, the antlered priest became the devil. In fact, he was a *shaman*, or magician-priest-doctor.

Graves came to an even more startling conclusion. He said that the ancients possessed a kind of knowledge based on intuition, on a certain oneness with Nature. This ancient knowledge sprang from the subconscious depths of the mind, and was symbolized by the moon.

When *The White Goddess* was published in 1948, many critics dismissed it as poetic fancy. Since then, however, an increasing number of scientific discoveries have supported Graves's ideas. Many scientists now accept that Stonehenge, Callanish, and other ancient monuments were intended as lunar observatories. The study of aboriginal tribes has confirmed the importance of the moon goddess and her connection with fertility rituals. In 1960 the anthropologist Charles Mountford studied tribes in the deserts of central Australia. He made a 300-mile journey with them to "centres of power", where certain rituals were performed. The ceremonies were designed to increase the life power of the worshippers, to stimulate the fertility of plants and animals, and to renew the sacred forces of the tribe. Mountford found that these centres of power lay on straight lines. Each tribe was responsible for looking after its own stretch of line, performing appropriate rituals to maintain its power. (According to students of dragon paths and leys, the lines of magnetic force do not remain permanently in the same place; they may change their location over the centuries, so that a holy place ceases to be holy.) Mountford observed that each centre of power was marked by a rock, and the Australian aborigines painted serpents – or dragons – on the rocks to symbolize the mysterious life force. However, the aborigines insist that it is not the painting that has magical or religious properties, but *the rock itself*.

Modern science is only just beginning to uncover the ancient systems of knowledge. It is therefore hardly surprising to find that there are dozens of strange and conflicting theories on the subject. The Austrian engineer and cosmologist Hanns Horbiger, who died in 1931, recognized the significance of the moon in ancient legends. He concluded that the earth has had several moons, all of which finally crashed into the earth and caused vast catastrophes like the biblical flood and the destruction of Atlantis. He was convinced that our present moon is a huge block of ice – a theory we now know to be untrue. The

witchcraft revival of recent years is based on the belief that
witchcraft is an ancient fertility religion, and that its forces can
be tapped today through the rituals performed at *Sabbats*, or
gatherings of witches.

T.C. Lethbridge thought that Stonehenge and similar monuments might be giant markers set up for the guidance of aircraft
or spacecraft. He also speculated that the moon might have
been the scene of a great war between two rival planetary races
– perhaps those of Venus and Mars – and that its craters were
formed by atomic bombardment rather than by meteorites. We
know that many of the moon's craters were created by some
kind of impact rather than by volcanic activity because they
sometimes overlap one another.

Lethbridge's theory sounds absurd. Yet in 1966 two moon
satellites – America's Orbiter-2 and the Soviet's Lunar-9 – both
photographed groups of solid *structures* in two different places
on the lunar surface. Ivan Sanderson writes: ''The Lunar-9
photographs, taken on 9 February, 1966, after the craft had
landed in the Ocean of Storms, reveal two straight lines of
equidistant stones that look like markers along an airport
runway. These circular stones are all identical, and are posi-

---

**Does a place of worship have more intense thought fields than
ordinary buildings? Can this explain the incredible case of the
doll with human hair that keeps on growing?**

The story comes from northern Japan and started in 1938. In
that year Eikichi Suzuki took a ceramic doll to the temple in the
village of Monji-Saiwai Cho for safekeeping. It had been a
treasured possession of his beloved sister Kiku, who had died
nineteen years before at the age of three. Suzuki kept it carefully
in a box with the ashes of his dead sister.

Suzuki went off to World War II and didn't return for the doll
until 1947. When he opened the box in the presence of the priest,
they discovered that the doll's hair had grown down to its
shoulders. A skin specialist from the Hokkaido University medical faculty said it was human hair.

The doll was placed on the altar, and its hair continued to
grow. It is still growing, and is now almost waist length. The
temple has become a place of pilgrimage for worshippers who
believe the doll is a spiritual link with Buddha.

The priest of Monji-Saiwai Cho thinks that the little girl's soul
somehow continues to live through the doll she loved so much.

tioned at an angle that produces a strong reflection from the sun, which would render them visible to a descending aircraft." The Soviet scientist Dr S. Ivanov notes that "the objects, as seen in 3-D, seem to be arranged according to some definite geometric laws."

The Orbiter-2 photographs, taken some 2000 miles away from the Soviet site, show what appear to be eight pointed obelisks. From the angle of the sun and the length of its shadow, the largest of these objects was estimated to be about seventy-five feet high and fifty feet wide at the base. This makes it sound more like a tall pyramid than an obelisk. Moreover, the Soviet scientist Alexander Abramov states that the distribution of the Orbiter-2 objects is similar to the plan of the Egyptian pyramids at Giza. A NASA official told Sanderson that the photographs were extremely clear, but explained that there had been "no speculation about them so far." He added that they had been filed.

On 26 November 1956 as American astronomer Robert E. Curtiss was photographing the moon's surface through a 16-inch reflector telescope, he was startled to observe a white cross near the ring plan Fra Mauro. Each arm of the cross was several miles long. Scientists have been unable to explain this phenomenon.

John O'Neil, science editor of the New York *Herald Tribune* observed a gigantic bridgelike structure in the Sea of Crises. The sun shone *under* it when it was at a low angle, making it clearly visible. Other astronomers have since confirmed the existence of this giant "bridge" on the moon.

These observations bring to mind the vast system of artificial lines that can be seen in the arid valleys near Nazca in Peru. These are a series of straight lines, interspersed with animal shapes and geometric patterns, that were scraped in the ground at some unknown date in the past. They look remarkably like landing strips for aircraft. They were not noticed until recent years because they can only be seen clearly from the air. The lines, which have been drawn in the rocky debris of the valleys, extend for over thirty miles, sometimes crossing ravines or stopping in front of small mountains and reemerging absolutely straight on the other side. The most puzzling question is how the lines were kept so straight by men working at ground level, presumably without guidance from the air. There are enormous designs of disks, flowers, spiders, and birds, which were only revealed by aerial surveys. On an aerial photograph they look like markings made in the sand by a child. The difference is that they must have taken hundreds of people hundreds of hours to construct. For what purpose? Von Däniken is convinced that they were markings to guide spacecraft; a likelier explanation is that they are connected with some ritual of the seasons.

If future astronauts can verify that there are artificial structures on the moon, built by intelligent creatures, it would certainly be one of the most exciting discoveries in the history of the human race. Yet even this would do little to solve the really baffling enigmas about our satellite. For thousands of years, people accepted that the human mind is influenced by the moon just as surely as the tides are. Our word "lunatic" stems from the age-old belief in a connection between the moon and madness. Then came the Age of Reason. Scientists and philosophers pointed out that the idea of a link between humans and the moon is absurd. How could a planetary body a quarter of a million miles away influence the human mind? It was a good point; but it was unsound. Modern research has shown that not only human beings, but also all kinds of animals, are affected by the moon. Oysters open and close their shells according to the rhythm of the tides, and it had always been assumed that this activity was the result of tidal movement alone. Dr Frank A. Brown, Professor of Biology at Northwestern University, found it to be otherwise. When he moved some oysters to a closed tank in the laboratory, away from the tidal influences, he discovered that they appear to open and close their shells in direct response to the movements of the moon.

The police have observed that crimes of violence tend to increase at the time of the full moon. One report from the Philadelphia Police Department stated that "people whose antisocial behaviour had psychotic roots – such as firebugs, kleptomaniacs, destructive drivers, and homicidal alcoholics – seemed to go on the rampage as the moon rounded, calming down as the moon waned." Nurses in mental institutions are familiar with the rise in violence and tension that occurs among their patients when the moon is full. Most family physicians in country areas, where the doctor-patient relationship tends to be closer and longer-lasting than in towns, can tell of people whose behaviour becomes eccentric at the time of the full moon. A doctor in the area where I live in Cornwall tells me he never expects to get an undisturbed night's sleep when the moon is full, and that there are far more cases of wife-beating and battered babies at that time.

How then, does the moon affect the human mind? The answer may lie in electrical forces. Scientists now know that the phases of the moon bring about modulations in the earth's electrical and magnetic fields. When Harold Burr of Yale University connected delicate voltameters to trees, he discovered that the electrical fields of the trees varied according to the seasons, to the activity of sunspots, and to the phases of the moon. The same delicate voltmeters connected to human beings are able to tell when women ovulate, and when people are suffering from cancer. It would therefore appear that human health is tied up with certain electrical forces in the body. The Chinese believe that these forces run in lines beneath the surface of the body, and the points at which they join are acupuncture points. Practitioners of acupuncture treat illness by stimulating these points with wooden splinters or metal needles. Western television teams have filmed surgical operations in China conducted on wide-awake patients who have been "anaesthetized" by means of one, or a few, needles inserted into the skin at acupuncture points. The patients appeared to feel no pain, and one of them smiled and joked as a tumor was removed from his stomach.

Acupuncture works, and it is gaining wider acceptance in the West. But Western science has not yet accepted the Chinese belief that the "meridians", or lines of force, that run through the human body are of basically the same nature as the dragon paths that extend over the earth. This seems altogether more difficult for the pragmatic Western intellect to acknowledge. After all, the earth is not a living creature.

Or is it? Sir Arthur Conan Doyle, the creator of Sherlock Holmes, once wrote a short novel called *The Day the Earth Screamed*. In it the hero, Professor Challenger, reaches the startling conclusion that the earth is alive. To prove his theory he drills a deep shaft through the earth's surface, and drops an enormous stake down it. The earth convulses and screams. In the light of modern knowledge, this idea is not so wildly improbable as it sounds. The earth has its fields of force just as human beings have. We speak of life-fields in human beings. Why not in the case of the earth? Perhaps the earth is not alive in the same sense that we are. But if some investigators are right, it often behaves as if it were.

This theory would offer an explanation of why certain spots

on the earth's surface seem to be blessed, while others are cursed. When sceptics read stories of miracles at holy places like Lourdes in France, Compostella in Spain, and Holywell in Wales, they are inclined to fall back on the explanation that faith, like hypnosis, can produce miraculous effects on the mind and body. Certainly most reports of amazing cures could be accounted for in this way. But some of the most astounding miracles involve things rather than people. Outside the old church of Arles-sur-Tech in southern France stands a marble sarcophagus that weeps – to the bafflement of modern science. It would probably be more accurate to say that the marble sweats. When the heavy lid of the sarcophagus is removed, water is seen to form in its inner surface. Usually the slab is held in place with iron bands. There is a small hole, large enough to insert a pipette, in the top edge of the sarcophagus. Through this hole the sarcophagus yields up on average about two pints of water per day. This water is reputed to have healing properties, and does not evaporate if left in an open vessel. In the past, the flow of water has amounted to many gallons at a time – more than the cubic capacity of the sarcophagus. There is no spring near the coffin, and the mystery cannot be explained by condensation. It is just another of those unsolved enigmas associated with holy places and objects.

The same is true of two bottles of blood that are kept in a small chapel next to Naples cathedral. It is the blood of St Januarius, who was martyred in 305 AD. Three times a year the blackened mass in the bottle changes color, and takes on the appearance of normal fresh blood. This has happened thousands of times – always on three religious feasts celebrated in May, September, and December. Careful investigation has revealed no evidence of trickery.

What is perhaps equally significant is that there have been occasions when the blood failed to liquefy. Why should that be so? The most plausible explanation is that the liquefaction somehow involves the faith of the worshippers, and that if this is insufficient to trigger the strange psycho-chemical reaction required, nothing happens. However, it is also possible that the earth forces that animate the spot are less strong at some times than at others. It would be interesting to have full astronomical data for the periods when the liquefaction failed to take place, and so be able to determine the exact position of the moon and the planets at the time.

But what would be most interesting of all would be to

understand the laws that govern the interaction between the vital forces of the earth and the vital forces of our subconscious. If we could discover that secret, we would have taken the first great step toward recovery of the lost knowledge of the ancients.

chapter nine

CREATURES FROM OTHER WORLDS?

*I*n February 1855 England was in the grip of an exceptionally icy winter. Even the West Country, where winters are seldom severe, was covered with a blanket of frozen snow. On the morning of 8 February Albert Brailford, the school principal of Topsham village in Devonshire, was intrigued to see a line of peculiar prints in the snow when he walked out of his front door. The prints were shaped like horseshoes, each about four inches long, and looked like they might have been made by a hoofed animal. The strange thing was that the prints were in a completely straight line, one in front of the other. It was as though the animal had been treading an invisible tightrope on its hind legs. Brailford followed the tracks along the street, and pointed them out to various acquaintances. The villagers agreed that the prints were unlike those of any known animal. As they tracked them through the fresh snow, the mystery deepened. The tracks stopped at a high garden wall, and continued on the other side. Yet the snow on top of the wall was undisturbed. It seemed that the creature had jumped the wall with one bound, or walked straight through it.

All along the South Devon coast for forty miles people discovered more of the mysterious tracks. In some places they went over rooftops. In one village they stopped at the door of a shed and reappeared at the back of it, emerging from a six-inch hole. The prints went up to a haystack, disappeared, and resumed on the other side. They stopped at one end of a drainpipe lying on the ground, and started again at the far end. The tracks always lay in a straight line, although they often doubled back on themselves.

News traveled slowly in those days. It was more than a week before Londoners learned of the sensational events in Devonshire. City sophisticates smiled at accounts of old ladies locking themselves in cottages while men armed with pitchforks and shotguns searched yards and barns for some unknown creature. They were amused at the country dwellers' belief that the tracks were the "Devil's footprints". To city dwellers it sounded like a typical rural storm-in-a-teacup. They surmised that the prints had been made by some animal, and that the superstitious country folk had interpreted them as the marks of the Devil himself. However, when more precise information began to appear, even Londoners had to admit that it was a strange story.

A Devon vicar and naturalist, who denied that there was a supernatural explanation, carefully measured the distance between the prints. He found it always to be exactly eight and a half inches. A fellow villager some distance away had measured the tracks in his garden, and also found them to be eight and a half inches apart. From this it appeared that there was only one creature involved. The oddest part was that the tracks extended over forty miles of coastline and, allowing for detours and deviations, extended for more than twice that distance. What small animal, if there was only one, could walk over eighty miles between dusk and dawn, climbing over roofs, and leaping over or walking through haystacks?

A famous naturalist, Sir Richard Owen, examined sketches of the tracks, and asserted that the prints had been made by a badger. Owen's badger presumably walked on its hind legs.

The likeliest explanation seemed to be that the tracks were made as a joke by some local prankster. But even supposing he wore special shoes with horseshoes attached to the soles, how did he vault walls, stride over rooftops, and cover eighty miles or so in a single night?

One of the correspondents of the *London Illustrated News* drew attention to a report made by the British explorer Sir James Ross in May 1840. Ross had anchored off the desolate Kerguelen Island in the Antarctic, and had been intrigued to find hoofprints in the snow. His party followed them for some distance until they vanished on rocky ground. There are no ponies on Kerguelen Island, or any other animal that could have made such prints.

The London *Times* for 14 March 1840 contains an account of
mysterious tracks in the Scottish Highlands. They had been
followed for twelve miles through the snow near Glenorchy,
and they sound identical to the Devil's footprints in Devon.
They were shaped like horseshoes, but gave the impression that
the creature who made them had been bounding or leaping
rather than trotting.

There are many accounts of Devil's hoofprints in old chroni-
cles, but sceptical historians have been inclined to treat them as
superstitious inventions. A typical example may be found in
the *Chronicum* of the Benedictine monk Flavellus of Épernay,
France. Describing a wild tempest that occurred in 943 AD he
writes that, "demons or horses were seen at the height of the
storm." Abbot Ralph of Coggeshall Abbey in Essex, England,
records that after a tremendous storm in July 1205, "certain
monstrous tracks were seen in several places, of a kind never
seen before. Men said they were the prints of demons." No
doubt many of these old stories are either inventions or
exaggerations of an actual event. But couldn't some of these
ancient chroniclers have been recording visitations similar to
the one in Devon?

One explanation of the Devon prints was suggested by
Morris K. Jessup, the ufologist mentioned earlier. Predicta-
bly, Jessup believed that the tracks were made by some kind
of flying craft. He draws attention to the report of one observer
that the prints were so clear-cut that they seemed to have been
stamped into the snow "as if made by a drill or mechanical
frame." Jessup suggests that the marks could have been made
by a low-flying craft that maintained its distance from the
ground by some kind of energy beam such as radar. This
would certainly explain how the prints continued over rooftops and passed over walls and haystacks. Yet it fails to explain
why the tracks often doubled back on themselves.

As we have seen, some ufologists have suggested that UFOs
may originate in another dimension – a space-time world
running parallel to our own. David Lang, the Tennessee
farmer who disappeared without trace, may have fallen into
this parallel dimension. If he could unwittingly fall into their
dimension, why should not creatures from the parallel world
accidently fall into ours? One of the most remarkable things
about the Devil's footprints in Devon is that they wandered
around for so many miles, as if the creature who made them
were looking for something. They strayed over or through

walls and across rooftops as if their owners were unfamiliar with our world.

It is interesting to note that the stories of demonic activity from Flavellus and Abbot Ralph both involve extremely violent storms, when electrical activity would have been unusually powerful. Remembering the strange behavior of compasses in the Bermuda Triangle and other Devil's graveyards, is it not conceivable that unusual magnetic fields might create a bridge between this world and a parallel universe?

It is now time to pause and survey some of the ground we have covered. As we look back over the mysteries considered in this book, we have to admit that no single explanation, or set of explanations, can accommodate all these strange phenomena.

On the night of 18 April 1962 at about 7.30 p.m. an explosion ripped across the Nevada sky. The flash was as bright as an atomic blast, and the noise shook the earth for miles. Was it an atom bomb test? A meteor? An enemy missile or aircraft? These logical questions were never answered by those who investigated the incident.

The first report of an odd UFO had come from Oneida, New York. Observers there saw a glowing red object moving west at a great altitude. It was too slow to be a missile, too high to be a plane. A meteor was ruled out because this object was tracked by radar, and meteors cannot be. As it moved west across the country, reports of it came in from the states of Kansas, Utah, Montana, New Mexico, Wyoming, Arizona, and California.

At some point the huge UFO landed near an electric power station in Eureka, Utah. Until it took off again, in its own time, the station was unable to operate at all.

The possibility that the explosion was from a nuclear test was denied by the Atomic Energy Commission. Its spokesmen said there was no atomic testing anywhere on the North American continent at that time.

Jet interceptors from the Air Defense Command pursued the UFO, but radar screens lost it about seventy miles northwest of Las Vegas. It was in that precise direction that the blast took place somewhere above the Mesquite Range.

Few people in the United States ever learned about this unusual event. Only the Las Vegas *Sun*, which was in the area of the explosion, carried the story. The news was otherwise suppressed by the Air Force.

Besides, there are many other types of enigmas that have not even been discussed. To touch briefly on a few, let us look first at poltergeist phenomena, about which I said a few words at the beginning of this book. In a famous case that took place in 1878 in Amherst, Nova Scotia, Esther Cox was the center of poltergeist manifestations. Objects flew through the air, spontaneous fires broke out, and an invisible spirit wrote on a wall: "Esther, you are mine to kill." Several witnesses were present with the young girl when the threat was written.

Then there is the closely related subject of demonic possession. When a possessed woman was exorcised by Theophilus Reisinger in Iowa in 1928, her body tore itself loose from the grip of several nuns who were trying to hold her down, rose through the air, and clung to the wall of the room close to the ceiling. Hundreds of similar cases have been recorded, some by modern psychologists. If these phenomena are caused by outside forces, it would certainly appear that such forces can sometimes be hostile to us human beings. It is of course possible that the forces originate in our own subconscious mind. In this case, the problem is equally baffling, because it suggests that a human being may possess several different personalities at different levels. There have been many astonishing cases of multiple personalities in which a person has suddenly lost his or her memory and been taken over by another personality. The second character has then performed actions that are completely foreign to the normal personality. In *Sybil*, a book by Flora Schreiber, the woman Sybil was taken over by no less than sixteen personalities. In which world do these personalities exist? Is the world of the subconscious mind one of the parallel worlds we have been discussing?

In a book called *Superminds*, the British physicist John Taylor discusses people like Uri Geller and Matthew Manning, who can bend spoons merely by stroking them and cause metal to fracture without even touching it. Taylor has observed many such psychics, including young children, in his laboratory. He has concluded that there is no trickery involved in their ability to bend metal or move objects at a distance. It is his opinion that their powers stem from some mysterious force, akin to magnetism, which is probably also involved in poltergeist activity. If the force of a child's mind can move small objects around Taylor's laboratory, is it not conceivable that a similar force might have been harnessed to raise the 1000-ton granite blocks of the temple at Baalbeck, or the immense monoliths of Stonehenge?

The hypothesis that we are simply dealing with unknown and impersonal forces that may originate in the human subconscious leaves far too many mysteries unexplained. It would not account for people vanishing without trace, nor the opposite of this – the appearance of mysterious strangers in our world.

In the eleventh century, two extraordinary children walked out of a cave at a place called Woolpit in Suffolk, England. The chronicler Abbot Ralph of Coggeshall describes them as follows: "They had all their members like those of other men, but in the color of their skin, they differed from all other mortals of our earth." Both children were green.

The boy grew sick and died, but the girl survived and slowly learned English. When she could talk, she explained that she and the boy had come from a land where there was no sunlight. One day they had wandered into a cavern while looking after sheep, and had lost their way. When they emerged into the unaccustomed sunlight of a strange world, they were terrified. The children had at first refused all food except green beans. The girl became used to other foods, however, and her skin slowly lost its green tint.

The most famous case of a strange person appearing in mysterious circumstances is that of Caspar Hauser. On 26 May 1828 a shambling teenage boy wandered into the Unschlitt Square in Nuremberg, Germany. Trembling and mumbling incoherently, he accosted a shoemaker and offered him a letter. When he was taken to the police station, another letter was found in his pocket. One letter purported to be from his mother, who said that the boy's name was Caspar, and that his father had been a soldier. The other was apparently from a poor labourer who had brought up the boy, and who asked that he be taken into the army. It was quickly established that both letters were fakes, written by the same person probably to cover up the boy's identity.

Asked to write his name, the boy wrote "Caspar Hauser." He was able to mumble a few words, but otherwise gave the impression of being imbecilic. It soon became clear, however, that Hauser was not an imbecile. Although he seemed totally ignorant of the world and of even the most everyday objects in it, he began to learn with a rapidity that proved he was highly intelligent. Within a few months, Caspar Hauser had learned enough German to explain what he knew of his former life. He said that for as long as he could recall, he had

lived in a tiny cell. When he awoke, he found bread and water
on the floor. Sometimes the water tasted bitter, and after
drinking it he fell into a deep sleep. When he woke up, he
had been washed and his nails had been cut. He was not
unhappy because he knew no other way of life.

Handbills were sent out all over Germany to try to establish
the boy's identity, but no one was able to throw any light on the
mystery. Professor Georg Daumer, who became Hauser's
guardian, discovered that the boy had an unusually acute
sense of smell, could see in the dark, and found daylight
painful to his eyes – all of which seemed to confirm his story.

In October 1829 Hauser was found unconscious and bleeding
on the floor of Daumer's celler. He had been attacked by an
unknown assailant who had struck him down with a club, and
possibly also tried to stab him.

During the next four years, Hauser had a number of guar-
dians. Finally an Englishman, Lord Charles Stanhope, moved
him from Nuremberg to the nearby town of Ansbach in
Bavaria. On 14 December 1833 Hauser staggered into his
house, bleeding heavily from a stab wound in his ribs. He
explained that a labourer had brought him a message asking
him to meet someone in the Hofgarten. There a man with dark
whiskers and a black cloak had asked him, "Are you Caspar
Hauser?" When he said yes, the man handed him a silk purse,
and then stabbed him in the side. The purse was found in the
Hofgarten, and contained an incoherent note signed MLO. It
said that Hauser would be able to identify his assailant, who
came from a place on the Bavarian border. The name of the
place was illegible. Hauser died on 17 December 1833 without
having been able to throw any light on the identity of his
murderer.

From the moment of his appearance in Nuremberg, contro-
versy had raged around Caspar Hauser. There were many
theories as to his origins, but most people believed that he was
the illegitimate son of some noble family, and had been kept a
prisoner to conceal the dishonour until he became too big to
remain locked away. Jacques Bergier, a French writer on the
occult, has another theory that is shared by many students of
enigmas. It would explain the mysterious appearance of the
green children as well as that of Caspar Hauser. Bergier
suggests that, for many centuries, the earth has been under
study by certain extraterrestrial intelligences. "In my opinion,"
be says, "after the period of simply auditing and recording

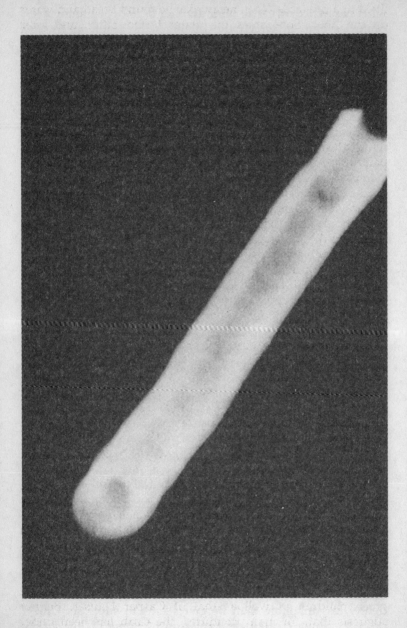

Unidentified flying object sighted over Palmero, Sicily 1978

what happened on earth, came another period, beginning a few centuries ago, in which the Intelligences began to conduct experiments. These experiments consist of introducing beings capable of arousing the most diverse reactions into our midst, and then studying the way we react – the way we study the behavior of rats in artificial labyrinths."

It is a suggestion worthy of Charles Fort. And, however great our revulsion at the idea of being treated as laboratory rats, it would certainly be hard to find a more all-embracing solution to the unexplained. Indeed, the chief objection to this theory is that it sounds *too* neat and easy. Any strange event can be explained by assuming that extraterrestrial intelligences wanted to study our reactions, and so deliberately engineered some incident that would baffle us.

There are, however, other mysteries that, if they do not contradict the extraterrestrial hypothesis, certainly challenge us to look for different possibilities. Two examples come to mind.

On 17 June 1908 an enormous meteor was seen to streak across the sky in Siberia. It struck the earth with a tremendous explosion near the Stoney Tunguska River. The explosion was heard for 600 miles around, and two villages were wiped out. But Siberia is a vast and barren land, and the government of the time had more to worry about than meteors – the country was seething with political discontent that led to the 1917 Revolution. In 1927 a scientific expedition penetrated the roadless terrain near the site of the explosion, and found that an area of 400 square miles had been devastated. The odd thing was that this meteor had not behaved like others. Instead of splitting into fragments as it hit earth, it had vanished like a huge bomb.

Later expeditions to the area also failed to solve the mystery. In 1975 a team of Soviet scientists concluded that the devastation had been caused by the tail of a comet that had struck the earth. However, students of enigmas point to an earlier finding that the soil in the devastated area was highly radioactive. It was as if a huge atomic bomb had exploded. Of course, atomic bombs do not streak across the sky. But UFOs do, according to all the evidence. Was it an atom-powered flying saucer that exploded over Siberia? If so, and if it was constructed by Bergier's extraterrestrial Intelligences, these beings are evidently less infallible than Bergier seems to suppose. Unless, of course, they created the explosion by some highly sophisticated means of remote control simply to see how people on earth would react.

If the aim of the extraterrestrials is to stimulate human beings for psychological study, it is hard to see what they achieved by disturbing a mausoleum on the island of Barbados. The Chase family tomb, which stands in a churchyard above Oistin's Bay, is constructed of stone blocks held together by cement, and is closed by a marble door. It was built in 1724 by a plantation owner, and his wife was the first to be entombed. It was not reopened until 1807, when the coffin of family member Thomasina Goddard was placed in it. The next year the massive marble door was opened again to receive the coffin of Mary Chase. She was the daughter of Thomas Chase, one of the most hated men in Barbados. In 1812 another of Chase's daughters, Dorcas, was buried in the tomb. According to rumor, Dorcas Chase had died through her father's ill-treatment.

A month later Thomas Chase himself died. When the tomb was opened to receive his body, some of the coffins were found to be disarranged. Mary Chase's coffin had been thrown across the tomb and stood upside down, and Thomasina Goddard's coffin was lying on its side. The family was indignant, assuming that hostile plantation workers were responsible. Other people were less certain. They knew it was unlike the superstitious Barbadians to disturb the dead. Besides, the marble door slab was heavy, and would have taken several men to remove it. Why would they have gone to all that trouble merely to overturn two coffins? The coffins were put in their proper places, and the vault was carefully sealed.

Four years later in 1816 the tomb was reopened for the interment of another child, Samuel Ames. It was discovered that all the coffins had been hurled about the vault. But the cement holding the great slab in place had been found undisturbed.

Two months later Samuel Ame's father died. A curious crowd accompanied the funeral procession to the tomb. When it was opened they were not disappointed. Once again the coffins had been thrown around the vaul – with the single exception of Mrs Goddard's. The Reverend Thomas Orderson conducted a careful search of the vault in an attempt to find the explanation. The tomb was dry and sound. There were no cracks either in the walls or floor. The seal of the door had not been broken.

The tomb was elaborately resealed. Three years later in July 1819 enormous crowds arrived to watch the interment of Mrs Thomasina Clarke. They saw five men chip off the cement from the slab, which was designed to open inward. Even when the cement had been removed, the slab seemed hard to move. The reason became clear when it had been shifted by main force. The leaden coffin of Thomas Chase lay against the door. The other coffins were once more in disarray – again with the exception of Mrs Goddard's.

After the vault had been searched in vain for any sign of intruders, the coffins were replaced, and white sand scattered all over the floor. The slab was again cemented into place, and then sealed with private seals.

During the following months visitors flocked to see the "haunted tomb". In April 1820 Sir Stapleton Cotton, the Governor of Barbados, became so curious about it that he decided to have it inspected. The seals were intact. But when the massive slab was moved, the usual disorder prevailed. Coffins had tumbled all over the vault. Mrs Goddard's coffin – now little more than a bundle of planks secured by wire – was the only one that was undisturbed. The sand on the floor bore no sign of footprints. The Governor decided that the strange affair was becoming a disgrace to the island. He ordered the coffins to be removed and buried. And from that day to this, the vault has remained empty.

None of the normal explanations is acceptable. An earthquake, to which the area is subject occasionally, would not account for the fact that Mrs Goddard's coffin always remained unmoved. A member of the Ames family believed that the answer lay in giant puffballs, a type of fungus that grows in caves in Honduras. These puffballs can reach a diameter of twenty feet, and can lift rocks by their thrust as they grow. On reaching their full growth they explode and disintegrate into powder. This explanation is improbable for many reasons. For one, Honduras is 2000 miles from Barbados. For another, puffballs had not been observed on the island. Finally, there were no cracks in the tomb for puffball spores to enter even if they had reached Barbados, and witnesses saw no sign of fungus between the stones.

It seems probably that, in this case, we are dealing with a mixture of poltergeist activity and haunting, centered around the coffin of the hated Thomas Chase. It would have been interesting to see what would have happened if Sir Stapleton Cotton had removed only Thomas Chase's coffin, resealed the tomb, and investigated it again later.

Clearly it seems unlikely that Bergier's extraterrestrials were involved in this curious mystery. But even as a haunting it was unusual. Normally poltergeist activities only take place in the presence of living human beings, as if they had to draw energy from a living person – or, as a psychologist might say, as if their energy originated in the subconscious mind. There have been cases in which poltergeists have persisted in the same house over a long period while a series of tenants have come and gone. This suggests that the poltergeist may be some kind of independent entity, a spirit, that needs to borrow energy before it can make itself heard or felt. There were plenty of human beings to supply energy for poltergeist activity in the area of the Chase family tomb. Many were simple peasants who were terrified of the phenomena. Their fear may have increased the psychic vibrations that led to the disturbances.

We must indulge in one more speculation in our attempt to formulate some general theory to cover enigmas and mysteries. The disappearance of Lang, Bathurst, and others suggest that there may be parallel worlds in our universe. Perhaps these worlds do not exist in other dimensions, but only on other

---

One day in August 1887 near the small village of Banjos, Spain, a boy and girl walked out of a cave. Some peasants working in a field saw them, and were utterly amazed. The two children had skin as green as grass!

When seen closer, the children were found to have almond-shaped eyes of an Asiatic type. They could not speak Spanish, and they wore clothes of a material never before seen in the Spain of the nineteenth century. No one could understand their language, and no one could analyze the fabric. For five days the boy and girl would not eat any of the various foods brought to them. Finally they began to eat beans. By then the boy was so weakened that he died, but the girl survived. The green color of her skin gradually faded.

After learning some Spanish, the girl described the country she came from and how she had left it. Her story only made the mystery deeper. She said her native land had no sun at all, and was separated from a sunny land by a river. One day a sudden whirlwind had lifted her and the boy and deposited them in the cave.

The green girl of Banjos lived for only five years more. The mystery of how she and the boy had appeared in Spain was never solved.

energy levels. Perhaps they can intermingle as the different levels of matter – solids, liquids, and gases – do in our world, as in a syphon of soda water, for example. If we look back over the scientific history of the past few hundred years – from Galileo to Einstein, from electricity to black holes – we cannot lightly dismiss Lethbridge's hypothesis that we live in a multi-level universe in which our reality is only one of many.

This book has been about the *interaction* of these levels of reality. Some people seem to have slipped through a "crack" in our reality into another world. Some phenomena – including poltergeists, UFOs, and lake monsters – seem to have slipped from some other level of reality into our world. It seems possible that certain types of powerful electrical phenomena are able to link the two worlds – and for all we know, the results may be as startling and incomprehensible to the inhabitants of these other worlds as they are to us. There is also a certain amount of evidence that some part of us – the psychic part – already has a bridge to other levels. This may be why certain people can foretell the future, or describe a crime simply by holding some object associated with it. Thought evidently has far more power than we give it credit for. It may be able to stamp itself on objects, leaving an imprint that remains for thousands of years. Some of the unknown forces we are trying to understand may be evil. Their thoughts may be able to evoke evil reality, as in the case of curses.

Imagine a book of unexplained mysteries written by a contemporary of Shakespeare. It might include the mystery of the falling stars that sweep through the sky foretelling disaster; the mystery of the Kraken, the giant sea devil with fifty foot tentacles; the mystery of monster bones, sometimes found in caves or on beaches. Such a book would be a curious mixture of truth and absurdity, fact and legend. We would all feel superior as we turned its pages and murmured: "Of course, they didn't know about comets and giant squids and dinosaurs." If *this* book should happen to find its way into the hands of our remote descendants, they may smile pityingly and say: "It's incredible to think that they knew nothing about epsilon fields or multiple psychic feedback or cross gravitational energies. They didn't even know about the ineluctability of time." But let us hope that such a descendant is in a charitable mood, and might add: "And yet they managed to ask a few of the right questions."